Rum Bullets and Cod Fish

Canadian Historical Mysteries – Nova Scotia
H. Paul Doucette

Print ISBNs
BWL Print 9780228624707
LSI Print 9780228624714
Amazon Print 9780228624721

Dedication

To the Past with many thanks

Acknowledgement

BWL Publishing Inc. acknowledges the Government of Canada and the Canada Book Fund for their financial support in creating the Canadian Historical Mysteries.

Canadian Historical Mysteries

Rum Bullets and Cod Fish - Nova Scotia

Sleuthing the Klondike – Yukon

Who Buried Sarah- New Brunswick

The Flying Dutchman – British Columbia

Bad Omen - Nunavut

Spectral Evidence – Newfoundland

The Seance Murders – Saskatchewan

The Canoe Brigade – Quebec

Discarded – Manitoba

Twice Hung - Prince Edward Island

Jessie James' Gold – Ontario

A Killer Whisky – Alberta

Table of Contents

"Prohibition didn't work in the Garden of Eden. Adam ate the apple."

Vicente Fox

Prologue

The November night sky was clear, black, moonless; the only lights a myriad of brilliant white stars glinting like so many pinholes in an ebony canvas. Beneath them the sea rolled with long three-to-five-foot swells pushed by a fresh nor'easter wind; which was unusual for this time of year. The small fishing boat plowed its way over the sea at ten knots, riding up and down with an easy roll.

Ken Joudrey stood at the wheel, his trained eyes looking from the small magnetic compass set in the frame of the woodwork to the window of the wheelhouse, straining to see any sign of a signal in the blackness.

"'Ere," he called without looking away. "You 'bout done?"

"Yeah," his younger brother, Bill, yelled as he finished pulling the heavy tarpaulin off the wood covered five by five hatch. "You see anythin' yet?"

"No. Hurry up an' git yer arse up forward to look out."

"Yeah, yeah, keep yer pants on."

The boat was a forty-five-foot inshore fisher powered by a rebuilt diesel motor out of Ingramport on St. Margaret's Bay. It usually trolled heavy cod lines for haddock and pollock from wooden casks set on deck, but it was getting harder to make a decent living from fish these days. Normally there would be at least four men on board. But not tonight. Tonight, they were not out here for the fish; tonight they were on their way to collect a bigger cargo and more money. Illegal liquor.

They had been running liquor from ships offshore for about seven months now and were doing quite well...so far. It was risky business running liquor, especially this far out from shore, with the constant pressure from the Canadian Customs patrol boats that were always trying to catch them.

"Everythin's ready," Bill said as he entered the tight wheelhouse.

"Good. Take the torch an' git up top an' start signallin'. Ya knows da drill," Ken said. "We should be close by now."

"Okay."

Ken reached for the throttle and pulled it back about a quarter of the way, slowing the boat to about eight knots. The boat responded quickly to the drop in speed by reacting to the swells more acutely.

A few minutes later, Ken spotted a quick glint of white light in the darkness. A second later, Bill banged on the roof. "Did ya see that? There, about three points off to da port."

"Got it," Ken called out as he pushed the throttle forward and steered for the light.

Ten minutes later, he was manoeuvring the boat alongside the schooner on the lee side. Bill tossed a bow line to a crewman on the schooner while Ken went and secured the stern. Almost at once, the work of transferring the cargo commenced as the schooner's crew began slinging cases of whisky and rum in cargo nets over the rail. Ken and his brother, with the help of two men from the ship, stowed the cases on deck in the shallow cargo space that normally held fish. Thirty minutes later, two hundred and twenty cases were piled on deck: twenty-six-hundred and forty bottles of booze at thirty dollars a bottle equaled seventy-nine thousand two hundred dollars. Bill and the two men covered the load with a heavy tarpaulin, securing it to the gunnels.

Ken was on the schooner with the captain. He had taken a strongbox filled with hundred-dollar banknotes from inside the boat's cabin and handed it to the man, who opened it and thumbed the notes.

"Looks okay," he said in a thick New England accent. He was obviously a Gloucester fisherman. "Good luck on yer run back."

"T'anks," Bill said. "By da by. Ya didn't see or 'ear any a CPS patrol boats did ya?"

"No. Least not in da last two days."

"Okay. I'll be away den."

He slipped over the rail, stepping on the covered cargo hatch cover and headed for the wheelhouse.

"Okay, Bill, let go lines."

Minutes later, he was increasing his speed and spinning the wheel to a heading that would take them towards Halifax Harbour and their final destination, a spot on the Northwest Arm. Within minutes the schooner dropped out of sight behind them. He looked down at the compass waiting for the heading he wanted before easing off the wheel. As was the custom when running the liquor, he left his running lights off until he saw the lights of the outer harbour buoys.

The boat was handling with more difficulty now that she was headed into the wind and battling the swells. It cut through the water at about seven knots due to the increased weight from the cargo. The trip would take just over an hour if everything stayed as is.

He was about twenty minutes into the run when his brother leaned inside the wheelhouse.

"We gots trouble," he said.

"What?" Ken asked, looking quickly over his shoulder.

"I t'ink dere's a patrol boat back dere. I 'eard its engine."

"Shit. Go back to the stern an' keep an eye open. Yell if ya see anythin'."

Bill disappeared as he pushed the throttle hard, trying to get a few more revolutions out of the motor.

Minutes later he heard Bill yelling from the stern. Then...his heart stuttered.

"This is CPS Patrol boat Beebe," a voice blared out of the darkness; the speaker obviously using a megaphone, as a beam of light suddenly lit up the stern. "Heave to and shut down your motor and prepare for inspection. If you do not comply, we will open fire."

"Jesus, Mary and Joseph," Bill said as he came into the wheelhouse. "Whadda we goin' to do?"

"No choice," Ken said, resigning himself to his fate. "Can't outrun 'im an' ain't 'nough time ta dump the cargo. Shit." He reached out a hand for the starter and flipped a switch, killing the motor.

He knew what he was facing. He had seen the Beebe soon after it was stationed in Ingramport. For now, his fate was in the hands of the law. He and his brother stepped outside the wheelhouse with their hands up just as the cutter eased alongside and three CPS officers scrambled over the rails. Two more men stood at the ready on the cutter, holding rifles.

Ken Joudrey stood silently as the men began to untie the secured tarpaulin. All he could think at that exact moment was someone in Halifax was about to have a bad night. An expensive bad night.

"It's liquor," one of the men said to the skipper on the cutter as he held up a bottle of dark rum. "Looks like a coupla hundred cases."

"Okay," the skipper said. "Cover it up and prepare to take the helm. We'll head for Halifax and turn this lot over to the Mounties."

"Aye, aye sir."

"You there," the skipper called to one of the men holding a rifle. "Bring those two on board and shackle them. Put them in the main cabin. I'll see to them once we get under way. Then go tell the radioman to report in that we're returning to port and request to have the RCMP waiting to take this load and these men into custody."

"Yes sir," one of the men said pushing the brothers toward the cutter.

As the two crossed over the rails Ken thought he heard someone say, "Looks like the informant was dead on."

Ken and Bill Joudrey were sitting on a leather settee with their backs against the bulkhead in the main cabin of the cutter. Their wrists were bound together with iron braces coupled by six inches of linked chain. A table was secured to the deck in front of them. On the opposite side of the table, a crewman sat staring at them. He had a pistol holster attached to his belt.

"This ain't yer night lads," he said with a smirk on his face, breaking the silence.

"Piss off," Bill snarled which caused Ken to kick him under the table, an unsubtle signal telling him to shut up.

The Sambro light flashed off the port side, signalling they were nearing the harbour entrance. The helmsman could just make out the outline of Point Pleasant at the southern tip of the city. He checked his heading, making sure he was in the channel. The other boat was forty feet astern and following in the cutter's wake.

"Make for the Government Wharf," the skipper ordered once they passed between George's Island and the seawall. He raised a pair of binoculars that hung around his neck. "Good. The Mounties are there with a truck."

An hour later, the Joudreys were sitting in a cold cell up in Rockhead Prison. They were formally charged with the smuggling of illegal contraband under the Prohibition Act and would face a judge later that day. Their precious cargo was off-loaded and taken to a secure warehouse to await destruction.

As it happened, just at the moment they were being processed into the prison two men were being let out. One of the men, Len Purcell, saw them, which was lucky for them since he also worked for Allister Fenwick as his middleman and knew Ken Joudrey. Purcell was waiting outside the gate for his ride to come and pick him up.

Once his ride arrived, he told the driver to get him to a telephone. The driver headed for a nearby corner grocer where Purcell got out and went inside.

"You got a phone?" he asked the old man behind the counter.

"There," the man said, pointing at the back wall.

Purcell headed for the phone and lifted the receiver off the hook and dialed.

"Boss," he said when the call was answered. "It's me, Lenny."

"What the hell are you doing calling me at this time of day?" Fenwick snapped.

"Look, I jus' got cut loose from da Rock an' I seen the Joudreys bein' taken inside in shackles."

"What? What did you say?"

"Da Joudreys. Dey been arrested."

"Damn it. Right. Listen closely. Nose around and see what you can learn then get back to me right away, do you understand?"

"Yeah."

"Go." Fenwick snapped and hung up.

He hung up and walked back to the front of the shop, pausing long enough to drop a dollar banknote on the counter. "Thanks."

Purcell called back around four o'clock.

"What did you learn?" Fenwick asked.

"Word is the CPS got a tip 'bout a boat makin' a run. Seems whoever spoke to them knew enough 'bout where the schooner was waitin' to make its delivery. Anyway, they captured the Joudreys with the whole shipment. One a' my mates sez he seen them off loadin' a coupla hundred cases down at the Government Wharf 'round 'bout eight this mornin'. The Mounties took the lot away in a truck."

"That's it?"

"Yeah," Purcell said.

"You say one of your contacts said something about the CPS being tipped off. How does he know that?"

"Knows one a' the crewmen on the cutter that captured them who sez they got a call."

"Did he say who made the call?"

"No."

"Okay. You did good. Keep your ears open for any more information and see if you can find where the Mounties took the cargo."

"Yes sir."

Fenwick hung up the phone and sat back in his chair. 'An informant,' he thought; 'odd, usually the people outside the city are quite helpful to the runners.' But, for now, the main problem he had to deal with was to try and find out where the cargo had been taken, and to get the Joudreys out of jail, which would be simple enough. All it needed was a phone call to his barrister. The other problem would require help from a higher authority. Fortunately he knew just who to call.

Chapter One

It was an unusually mild day for November, despite being overcast, probably because of the light wind blowing onshore from out of the southwest. Barrington Street was busy as usual with cars, trucks, and trams. Pedestrians crowded the sidewalks likely taking advantage of the fair weather to visit their favourite shops.

I had been summoned to Halifax by my boss, Walter McCarthy, head of the Customs Preventive Service on the east coast, headquartered here in Halifax. I was his main 'trouble shooter' in dealing with the rampant smuggling going on, especially in illegal liquor. My name is Jerome Conway, Jerry to my closer contacts. I was employed by the Canadian Government as a Customs agent however for the last couple of years I had worked exclusively for McCarthy as his personal investigator operating out of the small outports up and down the coast. But today, I was on my way to a special meeting at headquarters. I had new orders to report to Halifax for re-assignment to a new case, although I had no idea what it would be. The meeting was to be held at the Department of Marine and Fisheries building in Halifax.

* * *

I joined the Customs Preventive Service in 1920 shortly after the Americans declared their Prohibition Act. At the time I was employed with the Toronto Police with five years' service. Word had come around that a government agency was looking to hire men with police training. It was rumoured that this agency was a good place to work, offering more challenges and faster promotion than the police force, so I applied and was accepted. I was thirty-one at the time. Since signing on, I quickly proved myself and was promoted to Investigator.

Four men sat around the large oak table in the meeting room; two on one side, one sat opposite them, and the fourth man sat at the head of the table. The two men on one side were dressed in uniforms; one was with the Provincial Police, the other in the uniform of the Royal Canadian Mounted Police. The man sitting opposite them was dressed in mufti, as was the man sitting at the head of the table.

The man in mufti was John Lee; an American representing the Bureau of Prohibition which was attached to their Department of Justice. McCarthy, at the head of the table, was with the Canadian

18

Customs Preventive Service. He was the one responsible for calling this meeting.

Walter McCarthy was fifty-five with white hair and thick bushy eyebrows, he was a career civil servant and politician, a product of the English school system. At present, he was serving as the District Chief Preventive Officer for Halifax. He had been ordered to chair this meeting by his superiors in Ottawa.

At the moment there was a heated, and at times animated, discussion going on between the two police officers and the American. They were arguing over the problems arising from the illegal liquor business that was going on unchecked in both their countries.

"Gentlemen," McCarthy said, rapping his knuckles on the top of it. "This is getting us nowhere. We already know what the problems are and the need to find a solution. This is not the time for fighting over jurisdiction."

The three men stopped talking and turned to look at McCarthy.

"Alright," John Lee snapped. "What do you propose?"

"Yes sir," Phillip Jacobs, the Mountie added. "What do you suggest? Matt and I would really be interested." He was referring to the man beside him, Matt Murphy.

"Well, it just so happens that I may have an answer for all of you." He pushed a button on the intercom sitting on the table and a moment later the door opened, and a man stepped inside.

"Allow me to introduce Jerome Conway. He is one of our investigators currently working the St. Margaret's Bay area with numerous small fishing villages along its shores and key points of contact for the runners. I have called him here to meet with us because he will be the fifth member of our group. Take a seat," McCarthy said, gesturing me to an empty chair next to Lee. "The man sitting beside you is John Lee; an agent with the American Bureau of Prohibition. The others I believe you know."

I reached across the table and shook hands with Jacobs and Murphy then took Lee's hand as I sat down beside him.

"Now that everyone is here allow me to outline my plan," McCarthy said. "But first, I want each of you to read this before we begin."

He passed a copy of a single sheet of paper to each of us.

"As you see, two nights ago one of our cutters, acting on an anonymous tip, intercepted a runner carrying a significant amount of contraband alcohol that the runners received from a vessel sitting outside the three-mile limit. It is estimated to be valued at approximately eighty thousand dollars."

"Bloody hell," Murphy said.

"Quite so. I think that this might be just the break we have been waiting for."

"How so?" Lee asked, setting the piece of paper down.

"As you know, the biggest problem we have been dealing with has been the support these runners have been enjoying from the local communities, including here in the city."

"Uh-huh," Lee said. "We have a similar problem back in the States."

"True, but the difference is that the support here is voluntary, not coerced." He was alluding to the influence the mobsters and gangs exercised in the States. "As I was saying, we have an opportunity here to infiltrate their operations and perhaps even identify the key people at the top."

"I'm guessing that is why Mr. Conway is here?" Lee said, giving me the once over.

"Precisely. He is one of the Service's best investigators. And no one knows this traffic or trade better than him."

"Hmm. Okay. Tell us your plan."

I think now would be an excellent time for each of you to tell us what your involvement has been in dealing with the liquor trade. Perhaps you should start," McCarthy nodded to Phillip Jacobs.

"Right," Jacobs said, leaning forward. "Our main focus has been on shutting down the landing areas where the runners have been delivering the liquor. Unfortunately, we haven't been having a great deal of success: too many places, not enough ships, or manpower. In spite of that, we have managed to intercept and confiscate over ten thousand cases and barrels of liquor as well as seizing a number of boats so far this year. Most of the cargoes came from the French islands of St. Pierre and Miquelon off the southwestern coast of Newfoundland. Ottawa has been working with the French Government to deal with the problem on the islands. We have been working cooperatively with Matt here and the Provincial Police on trying to follow the liquor once it lands." He turned to look at Matt Murphy.

"That's right," Murphy said, taking over at this point. "Unfortunately, it has proven to be a difficult endeavour. These people are either well insulated within their various communities," he said, looking at McCarthy, "or they are well connected...politically."

"So what you're saying is you don't know who these people are?" Lee asked.

"Not exactly," Murphy continued. "We know some of the players, particularly in the small out ports and villages along the coast but, like I said, they are protected by their fellow fishermen and families. No one will talk. We know they're landing the liquor and caching it somewhere but so far, we haven't been able to get anything solid to make a case to take to the Crown Prosecutor."

"I believe your people have also experienced similar difficulties," McCarthy put in, looking at Lee.

"You could say that, yeah," Lee said. "But our situation is more dire than what you're facing here. Our main problem has been coming from the criminal gangs like you suggested, particularly, Capone and his bunch in Chicago. They have been organizing, and to a great extent have centralized their power and hold over the illegal liquor traffic, among other things...and they aren't afraid to use deadly force to maintain that power and control."

"So we've been hearing," Jacobs said. "Is it really that bad?"

"Worse. Which is why we're hoping that something can be done up here; before the liquor gets to the States."

"Well," McCarthy cut in, taking back the conversation, "as you are aware, here in Canada our legal system and laws are different; very similar to yours but still different. For example, we have a completely different attitude when it comes to guns and gun violence. That is not to say there is none, but it tends to be the exception and not the rule. That being said, I believe that what I am about to propose might bear fruit and, if not putting an end to the trade, we can curtail a significant portion of the criminals' apparent immunity to the weight of the law."

Everyone sat quietly waiting to hear his proposal, especially me, since it was beginning to look like I was going to be in the thick of it.

"Simply put, we attack the problem from the land side. To that end, I suggest setting up a small task force dedicated to exposing the links between the criminal element and those providing protection from capture and arrest. This group will be answerable to my office alone and will open investigations into these connections and compile the evidence to bring to the Crown Prosecutor for arrest warrants."

"We tried that in New Jersey last year," Lee said, cutting in. "We found our man floating in New York Harbour with a bullet in his head."

"That is regrettable," McCarthy said. "All the more reason that we must try and deal with the problem as a joint effort from this side of the border. We obviously cannot engage in any actions in the United States and nor should we. As I understand it, your agency along with others have been dragged into dealing with those who are actually engaged in the trade at the street level."

"That's right," Lee said. "Although there are some people trying to ferret out the corrupt politicians and others who are making the criminals' job easier while making ours more difficult."

"My thoughts exactly," McCarthy said. "I think that we have the same problem here and that is what I propose this group should be concentrating on. To that end, I have requested Mr. Conway here to join our little enterprise. I believe you have worked together before, Matt?"

"Yes sir," Murphy said. "We worked together down in Yarmouth about a year ago. Good to be working with you again." He nodded at me.

"Likewise," I said.

"Perhaps it might be instructive to hear a few words from Mr. Conway before we go on."

"I gather, from the little I've heard, your plan is to go after the top people running this business?"

"That is the general plan," McCarthy said.

"Good. It's about time we stop pussy footin' around these people simply because of who they are. I agree that they should be the targets of any investigation. It won't be easy, maybe even risky; some of these people are highly placed businessmen and government officials, maybe even a judge or two. Look, so far, we've been dealin' with the problem from the supply end of the business with varying degrees of success, but the source of the liquor is still out of our control and jurisdiction in most cases. I think you'll agree with me," I said, looking at Murphy and Jacobs who nodded, "we pretty much know who is doin' the transporting and who some of the runners are but not so much who is runnin' them or who owns the delivery ships."

"That's right," Jacobs said, nodding.

"So how do we tackle the problem?" Lee asked. "I take it you have a plan and it's going to involve the Bureau?" John Lee said, cutting in.

I looked at McCarthy.

"As a matter of fact, yes," McCarthy said. "Ottawa has been in touch with Washington, and they have agreed, that in this case, it would be to our mutual benefit to pool our resources and work together."

"Go on," Lee said, sounding wary.

"You see this as a problem?"

"Not really. In fact, I think something like this idea of yours should have been put together at the start."

"Excellent. Then we are agreed that we combine our respective resources and attack the problem by going after the people enabling their operations on this end?"

Everyone at the table nodded.

"I propose that this operation be undertaken with only those of us present here. I will direct the operation. Constables Murphy and Jacobs will handle the routine business of investigations and interceptions as usual. However, any intelligence or information will be reported to me alone. Mr. Conway here will do what he does best: infiltration and interrogation. He will report only to me. As for our American brother, I hope that we can count on his agency to provide any intelligence from the American side of the border."

"That won't be an issue," Lee said. "When I get back, I'll pull together the resources from the FBI, Treasury, and Customs. The only problem might come from my superiors."

"How so?" McCarthy asked.

"A lot of them are politicians which means they'll have their own agendas so to speak and will want to know what we're doing. Remember, to a politician information is leverage, power. And don't forget, there is a strong possibility that many of these people could be on the gang's payroll."

"Hmm, that could be an issue. Maybe we can work out something between Ottawa and Washington. Good. If we are all agreed, then let's prepare to adjourn for now. I'll put the plan in motion and advise Ottawa."

The meeting went on for another forty minutes during which time a general course of action was laid out. In broad terms it went as follows.

John Lee and his Bureau of Prohibition would be responsible for acquiring intelligence on the American side as to who the gangs were working with here in Nova Scotia. Matt and Phillip would continue their efforts at confiscations and seizures but would also try to source out any names of higher ups in government, business and the justice department who might be connected to the trade. For my part, I was to work independently by trying to infiltrate the operators running the liquor to establish a line back to those enabling the trade.

I glanced at the wall clock for the fifth time: it read 6:45. The meeting was just winding up, and everyone was heading out. McCarthy asked me to stay behind for a moment instructing me to wait outside with his secretary.

Nancy Slaunwhite was twenty-seven; five-foot-four in her stocking feet. She had thick light brown hair that framed her face beautifully, with high cheek bones and blue eyes. Despite the business-like clothes she wore, she had a slender and supple figure. We had known each for some time now. She joined the department about a year after I did.

"Looks like something big is brewing," she said, looking at me. "This is coming straight from the top." She said this as if it explained everything, which of course it did.

"So what's new in your life these days? Got yourself a fella yet?" I asked, making conversation. Actually, we had gone out to dinner once or twice before. I liked her…a lot, but she was a career woman determined to make a success of herself. I respected that about her although I thought it was a waste of a good woman. That kind of thinking would put the feminists on the warpath, I thought with a smile.

"No," she said, smiling. "You know, no time and besides, there aren't a lot of men who'd be happy with someone like me."

She was right, of course. There are not a lot of men, especially in this part of the country, who would accept an intelligent and independent woman like her.

"So that means you're free for a night out then?"

"Maybe," she said coyly. "Depends on what you have in mind."

I just smiled at her and enjoyed seeing the faint traces of a blush on her cheeks. As far as I knew, I was only the second or third man she had ever shared herself with.

McCarthy and John Lee exited the meeting room together at that moment.

"Where are you staying?" McCarthy asked him.

"At the Queen Hotel."

"Very good. One of the better establishments in the city. Are you free for dinner?"

"Yes, I am. What have you in mind?"

"I thought I would have you join me at my club. I believe tonight is fish night. Usually very good. We can have a quiet chat. Get to know each other a bit better."

"Sounds good to me. What time?"

"Let's say, seven," McCarthy said. "It's not far from here; an easy ten-minute walk from your hotel. Just go down to Hollis Street then head north. You won't miss it."

Thanks," Lee said as the two men shook hands. "Seven o'clock."

I was about to follow McCarthy when Nancy gestured with her hand. I glanced at her as she mouthed, "Eight o'clock."

I winked at her then left the office with a smile on my face as I thought of the night ahead.

"So what do you think of my plan?" McCarthy said when we entered his office.

Not bad...if it works," I answered, taking a seat in front of a small wooden desk.

I had worked on a couple of past assignments for him as his special agent. This was a fact that very few people knew about my job.

"Quite. I am trusting that you will do your usual best on this. What was your read on the others?"

"Matt Murphy is a very capable officer who also has a sharp brain in his head. Jacobs. I can only say that the word on him is he's very good at his job and has a reputation for having no tolerance for law breakers. I can't speak to Lee."

"Hm. That is my assessment on Murphy and Jacobs as well. According to information sent down from Ottawa, our American cousin has a formidable reputation within the Bureau of Prohibition, particularly in regard to his dealings with the gangs. Apparently, he has had two lethal encounters with them in the line of duty."

"Jesus," I said.

"Yes, well, to go on." McCarthy sniffed, he was a bit of a prude and somewhat religious, so he didn't take kindly to any profanity.

"Sorry," I said.

"The American Justice Department, in collaboration with sister agencies, has compiled a significant volume of intelligence information on the gangs, their leaders, and many of their soldiers. So he will be an invaluable source of information for identifying possible links to people here."

"That'd definitely help. If he can provide us with suspected contacts here it'll give me starting points."

"I agree. You will, of course, operate independently as always, with a free hand to pursue any line or lead you unearth with the full support of all resources at our disposal. I leave it to you how you will choose to involve Murphy and Jacobs, bearing in mind that our special relationship should remain between us."

"Yes sir, I understand. Do you want me to report in daily as usual?"

"Not this time, I think. Call only if you need something and have something specific to report. You will communicate directly with Miss Slaunwhite, as usual. Well, I think that about covers it for now. I have to make ready for my dinner with Mr. Lee. Good luck. Oh, before I forget, what cover name are you using?"

"Thought I'd stick with my own this time. No knows me here."

"As you think best. Thank you."

I headed out and as I passed Nancy's desk I winked again and said I'd pick her up at eight.

Chapter Two

In another part of the city three men sat in the well-appointed library of a house on Young Avenue in Halifax's south end. Rows of leather-bound tomes on a wide variety of subjects filled several shelves along one wall. In the middle of the room was set a large oak table around which were placed six matching chairs. A lamp was situated in the centre of the table with a large stained-glass shade. Several volumes sat unopened near the lamp. A half dozen upholstered, wing-back Morris chairs made up the remaining furnishings along with a mid-Georgian Chippendale styled side table laden with crystal decanters.

The men were seated in the plush upholstered wing back chairs with a small round table near to hand upon which sat a crystal decanter of aged Scotch whisky. Two of the men were dressed in tailored black pin-stripe suits and shirts with silk ties. The other, a white-haired man of about fifty-five, wore a deep red smoking jacket. His name was Allister Fenwick, and this was his home.

Fenwick was a very successful and influential businessman with various business interests – not all of them on the up-and-up. He was very well connected in the upper reaches of society, including many in the provincial government.

Born in Upper Canada in 1865 to a prominent family, he later was sent to England to study at Oxford University where he majored in business and economics. Shortly after returning home, he headed east to Nova Scotia with a letter of introduction from a notable English Lord addressed to the owner of an import company.

He married the owner's daughter, six years later and, as a wedding present from her father, he was advanced to the position of Vice President in charge of international sales. He took over the company upon his father-in law's death five years later. He was first contacted by a member of the Capone organization with a lucrative business opportunity involving the importing of illegal liquor from the French islands of St. Pierre and Miquelon and the Caribbean. He took the opportunity and subsequently became quite wealthy.

"What went wrong?" one of the men asked. There was no mistaking his distinctive accent; he was from Brooklyn, a borough of New York City.

"What do you mean?" Fenwick said, taking a sip of his French Cognac.

"Ya know what I goddamn mean," one of the men snapped. "We're payin' you good money for protection from the authorities."

Antony 'Tony' Caruso was a mobster working for Al Capone's organization in Chicago. The other man, Sammy O'Leary was from a Boston based Irish gang. Both men were hard cases with a number of killings to their credit. Their presence in Nova Scotia was to ensure that the illegal liquor continued to flow into their respective markets. The fact that the two men were together lent some weight to the rumour that Capone was trying to set up a criminal organization based in the States which he would be the head of.

"I know what you're paying me for, however, even though I have a wide network of contacts within the government and local law enforcement, even I cannot predict or prevent the actions of an overzealous police officer."

"So take care of him," Caruso said as if it were that simple.

"That is not how we handle these matters here. Shooting a law enforcement officer is simply not done, especially if that officer is a Mountie. It would be the same as you killing one of your federal agents."

"Whaddya mean? They're still just cops."

"The Royal Canadian Mounted Police is our national policing agency. Think of them as being like your US Marshall Service and the FBI combined. Killing one of them would bring down problems you could not imagine, and we do not need."

"Okay, I get it. But we can't afford to lose shipments as big as the last one. Something gotta be done," O'Leary said, joining the conversation.

"Something will be done," Fenwick said, looking at him. "I believe I have a solution that should take care of any more missteps like this last one."

Both men gave him a hard, dangerous look.

"It better," Caruso said, his voice full of menace; hard, cold. "Any more losses'll be on you. Understand?"

"Yes." Fenwick was smart enough to take the Italian's meaning and it sent a chill down his spine. He was being put on notice that they would not accept any more mistakes or screw ups. It was time to start looking out for himself.

Ten minutes later, he stood at the bay window in his sitting room, looking out onto the tree lined street as the two men drove away. The leaves were gone now, littering the street and surrounding properties. Looking at them reminded him of death. He was not feeling particularly happy at the moment, in fact, truth be told, he was feeling the cold chill of fear as he recalled the implied threat made by the two Americans gangsters. He was not accustomed to such a feeling, and it angered him; it was beneath him somehow to be afraid.

He knew when he decided to enter the seamier side of life that there would be risks but the lure of enormous tax-free profits was too great. And money meant everything: power, prestige, influence, position. These were things he knew all too well now. He was well connected professionally, as well as politically, and he had established many resources here and in places like Montreal, New York, and Chicago.

There would be certain risks dealing with the mobs in the United States but none that threatened his life...until now. Maybe it was time to reconsider his situation and look at stepping away, he thought just as a car drove past. 'Yes', he said to himself. It was time to call it a day, perhaps even consider returning to his ancestral home in England. He chuckled softly at the thought, thinking of the kind of reception he would receive.

He left England in his third year at Oxford under a cloud of scandal. At the time, he spent quite a bit of time availing himself of the seedier pleasures offered by the underworld: gambling, liquor, women. He had overextended himself at the tables at one point and ended up owing the house a substantial amount of money. When his father learned of it, he cut him off from his generous allowance. However, he was able to come to an arrangement with the criminals holding his markers that ultimately led to his discrete resignation from the college. A year later, he was inducted into the gang.

Then, in 1918, soon after the end of the war, he saw the coming of what would become the Prohibition Era and recognized an excellent money-making opportunity. He took his idea to his bosses and convinced them that they should get in on this now. They agreed and he was sent to Canada to set up the operation in Halifax. Within a year he had put together a plan and armed with enough capital backing, set out. Since then he had established a lucrative money-making operation worth millions of dollars, of which he took a generous cut.

His thoughts were interrupted by the sound of the door opening.

"Pardon the intrusion, sir," his manservant said as he stepped inside. He wore the uniform of a domestic servant: a white four button jacket, shirt with a black bow tie and black pressed pants, their cuffs just reaching the shined black shoes on his feet. "There's a telephone call for you. Shall I transfer it here?"

"Yes, thank you, Mark," Fenwick said, without turning around.

"Sir," the man said then quietly closed the door as he left.

* * *

The day following my meeting with McCarthy and a delightful night with Nancy, I was back in my room at the Waverley Inn on Barrington Street. Around ten-twenty the front desk rang. It was Nancy calling to say I was to come in to see McCarthy at two o'clock. Apparently, there was a development that had some bearing on our operation. I said I would be there. This meant I had time to look for a place to stay that was less conspicuous than the Waverley.

What I needed was a place where I would fit in with the locals. Then I would begin by getting in with some of the bootleggers to get a line on their suppliers. After that, figure out who was running them. Sounded easy enough, but I knew from past experience that not only was it not easy, but very risky, even dangerous.

I headed out and stopped a moment to strike up a conversation with the doorman: Ron Pottie; an Acadian Frenchman from a place called Arichat in Cape Breton. He was an affable older man always ready with a smile and a good word. I asked him if he knew where I might find decent rooms in town; not too rich or flashy, just clean and quiet. He directed me to a place owned by his brother. It was on Artz Street up by the Dockyard and close to the harbour. He said he would call ahead if I was interested.

I met with his brother's wife, Mrs. Elizabeth Pottie, an hour later. She was a matronly looking woman in her early fifties, full bodied with an ample bosom and a friendly face, rosy cheeked and all.

The room was on the second floor at the rear of the house with its own entrance at the top of a steep flight of stairs rising up from the backyard. It was clean with a single bed, dresser, small drop leaf side table with an ewer and basin on it. There was even an RCA radio.

Her husband was away fishing on the Grand Banks off Newfoundland at the moment. We settled on a fair rent which, for five more dollars a month, included home cooked meals. Hell, who was I to turn down a regular home and a cooked meal! We agreed on the rent and her conditions: no booze, no women. I said I would move in later – after my meeting with McCarthy.

I went back to the Inn and packed what little I had; I always travel light. I headed downstairs and checked out. I decided to have lunch before going to the office and took a corner table in the dining room. The waiter came over and took my order: a bowl of fish chowder, cup of coffee and fresh baked rolls. While I waited for my order to arrive, I took out the file of papers McCarthy gave me before I left his office the day before. They contained background information on local villains active in the booze trade as well as a few names of some of the city's more respectable residents that he believed were involved as well. I raised an eyebrow when I saw a few of the names on the list.

There were two judges, four sitting provincial MPs and at least a half dozen prominent members of the business community and a couple of city officials. Damn, I thought, this was not what I expected to see; bootleggers, local criminals and the like, yes, not the cream of the city's elite. I saw the waiter approach carrying a tray with my lunch and quickly closed the file, putting it back into my travel bag. The meeting with McCarthy was looking like it was going to be explosive.

Later, at Customs Headquarters office, I entered the outer office where McCarthy held forth. Nancy was at her usual place behind a desk next to the glass paneled office door with the word DIRECTOR stenciled on it. She graced me with an amazing smile when I stepped inside.

"Hi," I said, smiling back. I stepped up to the desk and dropped a piece of paper on it. "This is the address of a room I just rented for the duration. No phone. There's one in the house. Number's there as well."

"Thanks," she said, picking up the paper and slipping it in one of the drawers.

"Anything happen since yesterday?" I asked, nodding at the closed door.

"Nothing special. The American was here this morning to say good-by. He's heading back to Washington. Other than that...," she shrugged.

Just then a green light blinked on her phone, signaling that the boss was ready to see me.

"Later?" I asked with a smile.

"Maybe," she answered coyly as I turned and rapped on the glass then went in thinking happy thoughts. They didn't last long.

"Ah, Jerome," McCarthy said from behind a large oak desk. "Sit."

He gestured me to one of two thick leather chairs in front of the desk.

"Coffee?"

"No thanks sir."

"Have you looked over the file?"

"Yes, and I have to say it wasn't what I was expecting to see. Surely, these people can't be involved in this business?"

"Not involved, but suspected with good reason," he said. "I've had most of them under surveillance for some time now, discretely of course, and have satisfied myself that these particular people warrant more consideration. Especially the ones with an asterisk next to their names."

I did notice that four of the names had an asterisk next to them when I read the file earlier.

"However, these people will not be your primary concern. They are being handled from another direction. I gave you their names because you need to be aware of them in connection with your actual purpose here."

"Which is what, exactly?" I asked.

"As you will recall, at our last meeting I related to you and the others that one of our cutters based out of St. Margaret's Bay intercepted a runner two nights ago, resulting from on an anonymous tip. The load has been confiscated and the men, two brothers, are being held up in the city prison."

"I remember."

"Well, this could be an opportunity. To that end, I have taken steps to ensure they do not make bail or release with the Crown Attorney until I give the say so."

"Go on, I'm listening."

"I propose you make contact with these brothers and maneuver yourself into their confidence."

"Just like that," I said with a hint of sarcasm in my voice. I had worked with him long enough with a high record of successful investigations that I got away with a certain amount of impertinence.

"More or less, yes," he said, ignoring my tone of voice. "What I propose is to deliver you to the prison in shackles and placed in a cell in the same block as them. Your cover will be that you were caught trying to bring in a carload of illegal liquor from out of province."

"That's convenient. When and where exactly am I to be arrested?"

"This evening. You'll be stopped just outside the city by two of Jacobs men. Jacobs is aware of the ploy, of course, but not the arresting officers. You will be taken straight away to the prison."

Looks like Nancy was going to be disappointed, I thought, not to mention yours truly.

"Now listen carefully. I have reason to believe that the Joudreys, the brothers, are connected to someone very prominent in the city; a businessman or a politician, I'm not sure which, and reports have come in about certain underworld figures arriving here from New York in the last several days. I suspect that the local personage may be working with the Americans. If so, then you will need to establish that connection as well."

"Any names?"

"There was a list of names sent from Immigration at the entry point but none that stood out. I have asked John Lee to check the list against the various agencies in the States for possible identification."

"How will I contact you?" I asked.

"The usual way," he said.

The usual way was by telephone using a special number that only he, Nancy, and I knew.

"One more item. If you are successful and they take you in, remember that there is someone from their home base who turned them in. If you can find out who that person is, you may have an ally."

"Yes sir. That it?"

"Yes. Go to this address. There is a truck waiting for you. From there you'll drive to this location where you will load four thousand dollars worth of liquor. You'll be stopped just outside of Bedford. Good luck."

"Thank you, sir," I said, standing up and exiting the office.

Nancy looked up at me. I saw the disappointment on her face.

"No fun tonight?" she said, noting the look on my face.

"'Fraid not, baby. But we got a rain check, right?"

"Anytime. Be careful."

I had just enough time to return to my new room and let Mrs. Pottie know that I would be away for a few days on a job. I paid her for two weeks to keep the room available and as a place to leave some of my stuff. She didn't press me for information instead said she was happy I found work so quickly.

McCarthy had arranged for Phillip Jacobs to meet me at a location up in the north end of the city not far from my soon to

be new home: Rockhead Prison – McCarthy
had a warped sense of humour. I parked my
car on a side street and went to the corner to
wait for Jacobs. I didn't have to wait long. He
pulled up to the curb and stopped.

"Get in," Jacobs said, leaning toward the
open passenger window.

"What about my car?" I asked as he
pulled away.

"Where is it?"

"Back there on a side street."

"I'll have it picked up. Gimme the keys."

I handed him the keys and gave him a
brief description of the car.

"Where we goin'?"

"The truck is parked over by the
Northwest Arm. You'll head out on the Bay
Road which will take you to Highway Three
which will take you in the direction of
Yarmouth."

"Where will your people be to make the
arrest?"

"About a mile after you get on the
highway. By the way, are you armed?" he
asked.

"Yeah. Why?" I asked. "You think there'll
be trouble?"

"Not from my people but there have
been incidents in that part of the county."

"Like what?"

"Robberies; a couple of cases of
attempted hijackings. However, according to

our reports the targets seem to be trucks carrying regular trade goods."

"Is that a regular route for movin' the booze?"

"We think so. I know some of the runners make for Truro and beyond but most of the runs are to Yarmouth."

"Any armed violence?"

"Luckily not yet, although we've been told sometimes there have been weapons, mostly shotguns, hunting rifles, that sort of thing. In any case, I think you'd better leave your weapon with me. Don't worry," he said when he saw me hesitate, "it'll be with me when you get out the prison. You'll get it back then, okay?"

"Okay," I said, reluctantly handing him my M1911 .45 automatic gun butt first.

"Christ, where the hell did you get your hands on this cannon?"

"Souvenir from the war."

We arrived at an area where several transport trucks were parked near a small rail siding and loading dock. He stopped the car, we got out, and he led the way to a two-and-a-half-ton rig with a tarp covered half box.

"This is you. Here's the keys. Remember, my people will take you about a mile down the highway. Good luck. If everything goes well, I'll see you tomorrow at the prison."

"Yeah?" I asked, looking at him.

"I'll be one of the officers sent to interrogate you."

"Oh."

We shook hands then I got in the truck and started up the diesel motor and shifted into first gear.

Everything after that point went off as planned without a hitch.

I was stopped by a patrol car with three officers inside shortly after ten o'clock in the planned area. They shackled me up and unceremoniously dumped me in the back seat of the car while one of the men climbed into the truck and wheeled it around across the road and headed back to the city with us following behind.

Once we entered the city, the truck turned off onto another street. Our car continued in the direction of the prison. I could see the outline of the prison against the night sky. It was a daunting and foreboding place, more than enough to send chills through me.

The prison was built in the late eighteen hundreds on land acquired from a local farmer. It was constructed of granite and stone that had become weathered over time. An octagonal building section rose above the walls. Once we drove through the high gates, I could see two wings jutting out from the center building. I guessed these were where the cells were located. Large, barred windows extended across the face of each wing.

I was quickly processed and put into a prison uniform then escorted by two heavy set guards to a cell. It was big enough for one with a single cot and commode. The door was made of steel bars, leaving no privacy to the inmate. I could hear noises from some of the other cells; snoring, muttering and the like.

As soon as the guards locked me in and left, I stretched out on the cot and went to sleep. It had been a long day.

The guards returned at six in the morning, rapping their riot sticks on the cell bars. I rolled to a sitting position and shook my head. There should be a law against getting up this early, I thought as stood and did my business.

There were twelve of us in lock-up. Most were in on non-serious crimes ranging from public intoxication to burglary.

By six-fifteen we were hustled out of our cells and marched in line to the commissary for breakfast which was surprisingly good. It had to be since all inmates were required to work while incarcerated. I spotted the Joudreys easily enough; they looked so much alike. I made my way over to where they were sitting and sat down opposite them.

"You're new," Ken Joudrey said, opening the conversation. "When'd ya get here?"

"Last night," I said, scooping a forkful of scrambled eggs into my mouth.

"Yeah? What dey git ya for?"

"Who's askin?" I said, eyeing him.

"Take it easy," he said. "Jus' askin'. No 'arm meant."

I chewed on my food for a moment then swallowed. I picked up my tin cup of coffee.

"Caught runnin' a load a liquor jus' outside the city." I glanced over my shoulder checking on where the guards were. "Name's Conway."

"Joudrey," Ken said. "Dis one is my brother, Bill." Runnin' liquor ya say."

"Yeah. I got a deuce and a half I hire out. Got a call for from one a' my contacts sez someone's lookin' for someone to take a load ta Yarmouth. A C-note's in it. So..."

"Know who hired ya?" Bill asked, joining in.

"Nope. Didn't ask. Didn't wanna know, if ya get me. But a hundred bucks is a hundred bucks, right? I mean, a run ta Yarmouth pays what, fifty to eighty, ninety tops...maybe. I figured it was a special load. So? What's yer story?"

"We..." Bill started to say as his brother cut him off.

"Let's jus' say we got caught with sumthin' we shudna had," Ken said.

"Hey, ain't none a' my business," I said, throwing up my hands. "How long ya been in here?"

"A coupla days."

"No shit. I thought ya hadda go before a judge before they could lock ya up?"

"Guess they're busy," Bill said.

"You guys got a lawyer or sumthin'?"

"Da people we work for 'spose ta send someone," Bill said, ignoring the hard look from his brother.

"Don't mind him," Ken said. "E's got a big mouth."

"Yeah, well, at least ya got some help. Me, I'm on me own. I reckon I'm headin' for some hard time."

"You not workin' fer anybody?" Ken asked.

"I was workin' independent. More money. After this I jus' might go on a payroll with someone."

Ken eyed me as I finished my breakfast. It was clear he was working his way to a decision. After a few minutes passed, he leaned forward.

"In about an hour they'll be puttin' us to work. Stick close to me an' Bill 'ere. We been working down in da quarry. We can talk away from the guards."

"Yeah? 'Bout what?" I asked.

"A job. Now shut yer yap an' make sure ya git on the quarry detail."

There was a large open pit area on the Narrows side of the prison called the Rockhead Quarry. Male prisoners laboured there, crushing rock into an appropriate size for the city to use in many of its construction projects. The work area was a large open lot at the bottom of a high rock face. I saw a large crushing machine at the opposite end and a tractor. It was then that I noticed almost all the inmates were working with shovels and wheelbarrows.

As luck would have it, I was pulled from the line when we were marched to the yard area for work detail assignments. Turned out that a couple of detectives wanted to talk to me. I was escorted into the interview room where I saw two plainclothesmen waiting for me. One sat at the table while the other stood, leaning against the wall. I didn't recognize either of them, so they weren't part of Jacobs' crew which meant this was to be a real interview.

They were good and pressed me fairly hard right from the start, but I played my part and kept quiet. Forty minutes later, a guard was called in and told to take me away. I was taken out to the quarry where they handed me a shovel.

"Now git ta work," the guard said as he turned and left me alone. I scanned the area looking for the Joudreys. Once I spotted them, I slowly made my way across past several inmates who were loading wheelbarrows.

"Why'd they pull ya from da line?" Ken asked, pushing his shovel under a pile of crushed rock with his foot.

A coupla detectives wanted to know who I was workin' for an' where was takin' the stuff," I said, pushing my shovel beside his.

"Yeah?"

"They cut me loose once they knew I wasn't gonna talk. Ya said sumthin' 'bout a job?"

"I know sumbody might be interested in a good driver with his own rig."

"Ain't mine anymore," I said, spitting on the ground. "Confiscated it when they took me in."

"Don't ya go worryin' over dat. Dis guy's got pull. Git it back quick enough."

"I'm listenin'."

"Not 'ere, not now. Later when we git outta 'ere."

"Whaddya mean when we get outta 'ere?"

"Guy we work for has a lotta pull, like I said. He'll git us out. If ya wanna earn some real dosh an' git yer rig back, then join up wit' us. Okay?"

"If it gets me outta 'ere an' my rig back, then yeah, I'm okay with that," I said. "When ya figure all this'll happen?"

"Soon. Jus' stay close."

"Hey, you two," a guard yelled. "More work an' less talkin'."

"Yeah, yeah, keep yer pants on," Ken muttered. We went back to shoveling the crushed rock.

Step two complete.

Later that afternoon, the brothers were called to the warden's office. Twenty minutes later, the guard came for me. Turned out their lawyer finally arrived, and they convinced him to include me in the bail.

Step three complete.

Once we were processed out and given our street clothes, we left and were taken to a house in the city and told to stay put, someone would be there soon to talk to us.

The house was in the west end of the city. I couldn't get the street name, but it was a well-to-do neighbourhood judging from the look of the house. A two-story wooden building with a small, grassed front yard, a couple of oak trees and a low hedge fronting the sidewalk. We were greeted by a middle-aged couple and taken into the front parlor where we were told to wait. They offered us tea and sandwiches which we accepted. The lawyer left ten minutes after we arrived.

"How'd you manage to get that lawyer fella to spring me?" I asked after the couple finished serving us the refreshments.

"We tole him that the boss would be wantin' to talk to ya," Ken said. "'Sides, he's got people 'e knows, if ya get my drift."

"An' why would that be again?"

"He always needs good men, 'specially ones wit a truck who ain't particular 'bout what he's carryin'. Why?"

"No reason," I said. "Jus' curious. " 'Spose he pays good?"

"You won't have any complaints."

"Sounds good." I picked up a sandwich. It was sardine with a bit of mustard. Not a particular favorite of mine but beggars can't be choosers as they say.

"So? How long ya been workin' for this fella?" I asked casually.

"'Bout a year," Bill said, speaking for the first time since we got out of jail.

Ken shot him an angry look, then cut in, "Dat don't concern ya. If ya get on, you'll be runnin' on the road an' probably won't be seein' us agin."

I put up a hand and said, "Didn't mean ta pry."

"Yeah, okay," Ken said. "Cain't be too careful ya know."

"Whaddya figure we're doin' waitin' here?" I asked, changing the subject.

"Dunno," he said. "Never did this before. Guess we jus' hafta sit an' wait an' see."

We didn't have to wait long. Twenty minutes later we heard someone enter the house. The woman who brought us the tea and sandwiches opened the door to the parlour and a man stepped inside.

He was dressed in a black pinstripe suit, shirt, and a silk tie. He had a fedora on his head which he didn't remove. He looked Italian, which meant the mob. I sensed an air of death about him. I had seen men like him before: mean; dangerous.

"You two the Joudreys?" he asked, looking directly at the brothers. I immediately picked up on his Brooklyn accent.

"Yeah," Ken said. "Who's askin'?" It was clear he had no idea the danger he was in. They had just lost a valuable shipment of alcohol, and someone was not very happy about it.

It was just possible that this man was here to find out why or to kill them.

The man ignored the question and turned his eyes on me.

"Who da fuck is dis?"

"He's wit us. We figured da boss could use a good man wit his own truck," Bill said.

"Hey, buddy," Ken said. "Who da 'ell are ya? Did da boss send ya?"

"All you gotta know for now is I'm the man ya gotta talk to. Now. Tell me exactly what happened to our shipment?"

"We got stopped by da Customs cutter," Ken said.

"Why didn't ya make a run for it?"

"Da boat was to heavy an' it was da Beebee what was chasin' us."

"What's this Beebee?"

"Customs cutter outta Halifax an' da Bay."

"Don't you usually know where the customs boats are before ya pick up da cargo?"

"Yeah," Ken said. "Only dis time we musta been told the wrong information."

"Where do ya get this information?"

"A cousin works at one a' da radio stations down in da Bay. 'E knows where da cutters are."

"So he's da one who gave you the wrong information?" the man asked; his voice full of menace.

"Looks dat way, but I tell straight, he's no sellout."

"You willin' to stake yer life on dat?"

"Damn right."

The man paused for several moments then, turning back to me, asked, "What were you in for?"

"Runnin' a truckload booze from Halifax," I said.

"Who for?"

"Dunno. Didn't wanna know."

"They say you have yer own rig?"

"That's right. A Ford deuce and a half ragtop. Although, I ain't got it no more. It was seized when the cops picked me up."

"Don't worry 'bout that. We can get it back. If we do dat means you'll come work for us, got it?"

"Depends."

"Yeah? On what?"

"Dough."

He stared at me for a moment. "Okay. There'll be plenty of dough you play yer cards right.

"Then I'm in."

He nodded slightly then turned back to the brothers. "You two can take off an' head back to where ya come from. Your boat is down at pier twenty-one. When you get back, I want you to nose 'round an' see if ya pick up anythin' might point to someone who ratted ya out to Customs."

"Ya t'ink someone..." Ken started to ask.

"Don't know," the mobster said, looking at him. "Jus' seems strange dat cutter turnin' up at jus' the right moment."

"Jesus. Ain't got no idea who wudda done sumthin' like dat. Most folk down home are related, see."

"I don't give a shit 'bout dat. Jus' look, got it?"

"Yeah, yeah, sure."

"Good. Now take off. Yer boat is down at dat government dock."

"T'anks," Ken said as he and Bill stood up and headed for the door.

After the Joudreys left, Caruso turned back to me.

"Talk ta me," he said, coming back to me. He sat down on the chair recently held by Ken Joudrey and pulled out a .45 automatic, setting it on the small table between us.

"Whaddya wanna know?"

"You figure it out."

Twenty minutes later, he re-holstered his gun and stood up. I gave him the prepared background story I had and where I was staying along with a phone number.

"Go back to yer rooms an' wait dere. We'll be in touch."

Chapter Three

Walter McCarthy sat behind his desk pouring over the latest reports from the Patrol Cutters. The information did not look promising: too many ships waiting offshore just outside the legal limit, too many fishermen running between them and the coast, not enough cutters fast enough to intercept them. The idea of Prohibition he understood, however, he felt increasingly frustrated by the lack of support from the government that demanded he put an end to the illegal traffic. He dropped the last page in his hand and turned to look out the window behind him.

It was another dreary day; overcast, wet and cold. A brief smile creased his face as he thought the weather was appropriate today. Then, at that moment a woman's voice sounded from the intercom on his desk.

"Sir," she said, "a call from Washington on the line."

He turned back to his desk and reached out to the intercom, depressing a switch.

"Thank you, Miss Slaunwhite." He then reached for his phone.

"McCarthy," he said into the mouthpiece.

"Walter," John Lee said. "Did I catch you at a bad time?"

"Not really. I have been going over the latest reports from our offshore services. It doesn't look too good. We have some moderate successes, of course, but not nearly enough."

"We have the same problem down here. But that's not why I'm calling. I received a call from one of contacts at the Bureau. It looks like two mob men have been reported headed for your area. They might even be there already."

"I see. That's all I need; the mob here."

"They were able to get their names and general descriptions. The Bureau has records on both men. It doesn't look good, I'm afraid. Both men are serious gangsters with several killings credited to them. One of them is from Chicago via New York. Name of Antony Caruso, aka Tony. The other one is from one of the Boston Irish gangs. His name is Liam O'Leary. According to the FBI and our border services, they crossed over into Canada four days ago in Montreal."

"And you say they are supposed to be here in Halifax?"

"That is the consensus."

"Hmm. Conway will have to be alerted to their presence," McCarthy more to himself than to Lee.

"How is that part of your operation going by the way?"

"He was picked up and jailed a couple of days ago. He was put in the same cell block with two brothers who were intercepted several days ago running a boat load of liquor. If I know my man, he has probably made contact with them by now."

"I hope you get the word to him about Caruso and O'Leary. It's a good bet if they're in your backyard, they're there on business. Maybe even with one of the principal players up there. If so, then this would be an excellent opportunity."

"Yes, I agree. Conway is very capable of handling himself, however, I will definitely alert him all the same."

"Something else to consider. If they are there to meet with their Canadian partner, then this last capture isn't going to sit well with them. These people aren't forgiving, especially if it costs them money. So be prepared for the possibility of bodies turning up. Might be a good idea to give a head's up to that Mountie, what was his name, oh yeah, Jacobs."

"Good idea," McCarthy said. "I'll alert him right away. Is that it?"

"Yes, for now," Lee said. "I'll be in touch as more information comes in. Good luck."

"Thank you." McCarty hung up the phone then depressed the button on the intercom. "Miss Slaunwhite, will you come in here, please?"

A moment later Nancy Slaunwhite stepped into the office, notepad and pencil in hand. She came over to the front of the desk and sat down.

"First thing, get hold of Constable Jacobs at the RCMP office. Next, take this down and pass it along to Conway when he checks in."

I gave a detailed account of the call with Lee concerning the two American gangsters.

"Oh my," she said when she finished writing. "Does this mean he's in danger?"

"I don't think so," he said, noting the look of concern on her face. "But it is best to be aware of the situation and to be prepared. He will be fine. He is a very capable person, as we both know very well."

"Yes sir," she said, standing up. "I will get Constable Jacobs right away."

"Oh, you better call Matt Murphy as well, but Jacobs first."

"Yes sir."

She managed to reach Constable Jacobs on her first try.

"This is Mr. McCarthy's secretary," she said when he came online. "He needs to speak with you. One moment, please, while I transfer the call."

"Ah, good," McCarthy said when he picked up. "She was able to get hold of you."

"She was lucky," Jacobs said. "I just about to head out. What's up?"

"I received a call from our American cousin. It appears there may be two known and dangerous gangsters in our city. They may be here to meet with the local contact for their liquor shipments. However, my main concern at the moment is what they might try when they learn of the recent loss of product. As Lee pointed out, these people aren't known for their forgiving natures."

"True. Did he manage to give you any details?"

"Yes." McCarthy then related the names and descriptions of Caruso and O'Leary.

"Does your man Conway know?"

"Not yet. He has not reported in. On that point I think in light of the present danger these men pose, we might be well advised to make an adjustment to our strategy."

"What have you mind?"

"Perhaps adding one more member to our team to serve as his back up, so to speak."

"Good idea," Jacobs said after a brief pause. "However, I don't think we should start adding more people."

"Oh?" McCarthy asked curiously.

"The more people we add, the greater the risk of something leaking out about what we're up to. No. I think you're right about covering him, but we should do it with the resources we already have."

"Do I detect an idea?"

"Yes. Why don't we put Matt Murphy on it. Maybe insert him as Conway's helper on the truck? Or something like that."

"That's an excellent idea. I leave it to you to work out the details. Conway is staying at rooms up near the dockyard." He gave Jacobs the address and phone number of Conway's residence. "I will pass this along when he reports in. I think it best you call him instead of him having your number."

"Okay. Leave it with me. In the meantime, I'll have my people begin watching for those two men."

"Good. But no one is to approach them at this time, yes?"

"Of course. I'll keep you updated."

"I as well," McCarthy said. "Goodbye."

* * *

Ten minutes after my meeting with Caruso I was on the street, walking in the general direction of my lodging. I was careful to watch for any sign of being followed or watched. I spotted a corner chemist shop up ahead and went inside. I asked for a pack of cigarettes and if they had a phone I could use.

The clerk gave me a pack of Player's Navy Cut and pointed to the end of the counter where I saw a black rotary phone. I paid for the cigarettes and stepped to the end of the counter. After a quick look through the plate glass window at the entrance to make sure there was nothing familiar outside, I picked up the phone and dialed.

"Mr. McCarthy's office," Nancy said into my ear. The sound of her voice triggered a very nice memory.

"It's me," I said, all business now.

"Oh, good. I was hoping you'd call." She sounded serious.

"Oh? What's up?"

"We had a call from John Lee, the man from the Prohibition Bureau in the States?"

"Yeah? And?"

"Lee informed us that according to his sources there are two known gangsters reportedly here in Halifax. According to him these men are dangerous and known killers." She gave me their names and descriptions.

"Yeah. I already met one of them; Caruso."

I gave her a detailed run down on everything that happened since our last meeting.

"It looks like I'm going to get on in the inside of their operation. Tell the boss I still have no idea who's running things yet or how their operation is set up. Also, let him know that the Joudreys are out and have their boat back. They've been ordered to go back home. It looks like these people think there's a rat in the woodpile, so if he knows who this informer is, he better take steps to cover him. If Caruso finds out who it is I wouldn't give a plug nickel for him seeing a new day."

"Okay," she said. "Just you be careful." I thought I detected something in her voice.

"My middle name, baby" I said. "Right. I better get going. Caruso said he was going to call me. I'll check in tomorrow if I get the chance."

"Okay." Then the line went dead.

* * *

Nancy got up and went to McCarty's office, rapping on the glass panel as she opened the door.

"Jerome just called," she said. He gestured for her to sit down. She repeated his report in precise detail from her notes in the pad she always carried.

"Very good," McCarthy said when she finished. "Looks like he's penetrated their operation, at least as far as passed the front door.

"Have you had any luck reaching Jacobs?"

"He's on patrol," she answered. "I left a message for him to call me. I took the liberty of not mentioning your name since you want this to be an in-house operation."

"Very good thinking. Put him through as soon as he calls."

"Yes sir," she said, standing up and returning to her desk.

* * *

The call came in a six-thirty. I had just finished a delicious fish chowder with fresh made biscuits with my landlady. I was in my room enjoying the last of the tea she made when she tapped softly on the door to my room.

"There's a call for you, Mr. Conway," she said from the other side of the door.

"Thanks," I called out. "I'll be right there."

I got up and headed down the hall to where a candlestick phone sat on a small end table. I lifted the earpiece that lay beside the rotary dial and leaned close to the mouthpiece.

"Yeah?" I said. I knew who it would be.

"Be at the corner of..." There was a brief pause, and I heard a muffled voice in the background, then, "the corner of Barrington an' Proctor at noon tomorrow. Watch for a black Talbot. Get in, keep yer mouth shut. Got it?"

"Got it," I said and depressing the hook on the side, disconnecting the call. I realized from the accent that it wasn't Caruso.

I checked to make sure Mrs. Pottie wasn't in earshot then picked up the earpiece again and dialed. I knew McCarthy worked well into the evening, so I was sure he'd pick up.

He did...on the third ring.

"It's me," I said. "I just got a call from one of the gang's people. I'm to be picked up tomorrow evening at six. I'm guessing they're taking' me to meet somebody. It's lookin' like the plan is starting to come together."

"And they gave you no idea what this was to be about," he asked when I finished.

"Nothin'."

"Hm. I think you are right about the plan working, although I am not overly comfortable with you going into a meeting not knowing what it is about."

"Them's the chances," I said. "I figure it'll be one of two things: one, they want to know more about me; or two, they got somethin' they want me to do."

"Sounds reasonable."

"If it is about putting me to work, it might be a good idea to be on the lookout for anyone trying to release that truck I was using when they arrested me."

"Why? Do you think they would try and get their hands on it? I do not see..."

"I told them that it 's my truck. They offered to get it back for me as part of their offer to join up."

"Good idea. I will take steps immediately to ensure I am notified of such a move. I will have Miss Slaunwhite call you. If you are unavailable, she will leave word of some sort at your lodging. Agreed?"

"Agreed," I said then hung up and returned to my room.

I had to admit I wasn't too happy about going into an unknown situation without my gun. Jacobs still had it. I'd have to make a point of getting it back as soon as possible.

The next day I arrived at the rendezvous point ten minutes early and was standing there, leaning against the stop sign smoking a cigarette, when I spotted the Talbot coming down the street. It slowed as it neared me then came to a stop. The driver leaned across and cranked the passenger side window down a crack.

"You Conway?"

"Yeah," I said.

"Git in."

I flicked the cigarette into the street then got in as instructed. The driver eased the clutch out and the car started to roll away before the door was closed.

We drove north along Barrington Street then turned onto Kenny Street. I saw the truck I was driving when they picked me up parked beside the curb in front of a single-story wooden house. My hunch was right. I guess McCarthy didn't get the word soon enough.

'Jesus', I thought, 'that was quick'. Whoever was running this operation must be really well positioned to have that much influence.

The driver pulled into the gravel space at the side of the house and turned off the motor.

"Out," he said. "We're 'ere."

"Now what?" I asked.

"Inside." He gestured for me follow him.

We went in through the front door. Inside, he signaled for me to head down the hall toward the kitchen at the rear of the house. As I neared the door, I noticed a wooden table with three chairs around it. There was a large pot sitting on it along with a couple of mugs.

"Take a seat," my guardian said, "'help yourself to a coffee."

I sat down on one of the wooden chairs, ignoring the coffee. I pulled out my cigarettes and extracted one, lighting it with a match. Buddy stood vigil at the door, leaning against the jamb. It wasn't long before I heard footsteps coming down the hall behind me.

"You see yer truck outside?" a man said when he came in and sat across from me.

"Yeah," I said. "I won't ask how ya managed to get it back."

"Smart fella. So you still wanna work for us?"

"That's why I'm here," I said, taking a pull on the cigarette.

"Good. My name's Lenny Purcell. I'm the one that'll be puttin' ya work."

"Okay by me," I said. "What's in it fer me?"

"Ya mean besides gittin' yer truck back?"

"Yeah, besides that," I said.

"Two hundred a trip."

"Plus gas?"

"Yeah, okay. Plus gas. This is your chance to show us if you got what we're lookin' for. There's a shipment comin' in up in Cape Breton outside Glace Bay later tonight. You hafta pick it up an' deliver it to a place in Eastern Passage by tomorrow morning. Think ya can handle that?"

"Yeah. No problem. That's a long haul, maybe seven hours up and, dependin' on how heavy the load is, maybe eight, nine hours comin' back. How big a load?"

"Two hundred cases plus a half dozen barrels."

"Yeah, eight, ten-hour return trip," I said, calculating for the weight.

"I'll be ridin' along wit ya ta help out with the drivin'. I know where to go both ends."

"The company'll be good. You done much long distance driving?"

"Don't worry 'bout dat," Purcell said, "I've done enough."

I figured this would a good time for introductions.

"Jerome Conway," I said, offering him my hand. "Glad to have ya ridin' with me."

He accepted my hand. He had a solid and firm handshake, and I could feel the roughness of his palm. He was definitely used to hard work: probably fishing.

"When do we head out?" I asked.

"No later than three o'clock. We'll be driving straight through both ways," he said, standing up. He pulled out a large envelope and handed it to me.

"What's this?" I asked.

"Half your payment. You get the rest when the job's done."

I opened the envelope and fingered through the banknotes inside: all twenties.

"Here," he said, taking his hand out of his pocket. It held a small wad of more banknotes. He peeled off three twenties and passed them to me. "Gas an' meals."

"Thanks," I said taking the notes.

"You need more, let me know." He put the wad back in his pocket. "The truck is gassed an' ready to roll. After we make the delivery, you'll come back to the city an' drop me off. If everythin' goes good, you'll be hearin' from us again for more runs. By the way, ya carryin'?"

"If I need to, why? You expectin' trouble?" I asked.

"Never can tell. Been a coupla attempted hijackin's lately. If ya got your own hardware best ya take it along. That gonna be a problem?"

"Don't know. I wasn't expectin' to sign on where I might hafta kill someone."

"Then don't get stopped."

Shit, why didn't I think of that, I thought, but kept my mouth shut.

I made arrangements to pick Lenny up at two-thirty down by shipyard then headed for the truck. I made it back to my digs and once inside called McCarthy.

"Looks like I'm in," I said. "I'm on my way up to Glace Bay in an hour or two to pick up a shipment for delivery back here somewhere over in Eastern Passage."

"Very good," he said. "Very, very good. Have you learned who is running the operation yet?"

"I met with someone named Lenny Purcell who seems to be running this part of the operation, but I didn't get the feeling he was the top man."

"Oh? How so?"

"Call it a gut feeling. He just didn't come across as someone with the kind of pull to get me outta jail and get the truck back."

"I see. Well, I trust your instincts. Now, what about this shipment?"

"Three hundred cases being landed outside Glace Bay sometime tonight. I'm guessing it's coming in from the French islands."

"Most probably. Are you going up there alone?"

"No. Purcell's ridin' with me; supposedly as a second driver and paymaster. Oh yeah, another thing, it was suggested that I carry a weapon."

"They must expect trouble?"

"Don't know, but we do know that there have been a number of attempted hijackings by rival operators lately. My main concern is what might happen if the local constabulary stops us."

"Quite so. I will have to alert Constables Jacobs and Murphy to bring them up to date. I am sure they can make the necessary arrangements to lessen that possibility."

"Good. Also, if you can reach Jacobs before two o'clock, tell him I'd like my gun back. He can deliver it to me at my digs."

"Is that all?" he asked.

"For now, yeah. I'll check in after I get back," I said.

"Make sure you get names when you are up there, particularly, the name of the boat and any crewmen."

"Yes sir."

"Have a safe trip. Good luck." He hung up.

It was an hour after talking with McCarthy when Mrs. Pottie called me to the phone again. This time it was Jacobs.

"Hi," he said when I picked up. "Hear things are moving right along?"

"Yeah," I said. "Looks that way. McCarthy tell you everything?"

"More or less, yeah, unless you have anything new to add?"

"Not yet. I'll be headin' out soon to pick up my minder, a fella named, Lenny Purcell.

I think he's a local fisherman lookin' for extra dosh like most a' them these days."

"I'll check him out. McCarthy said you also reported there might be a possibility of gun play. What's that about?"

"Not sure, but as you probably know already, there's been reports of attempted hijackin's by rival operators. That's not my main worry, though. Goes with the territory. It's the possibility of a run in with any of your people or Murphy's. I don't know how far Purcell will go if we're stopped by any police. Mind you, if it comes to it, I can and will deal with it. But it would help if you can somehow see to it we get a free ride."

"I'll see what I can do," Jacobs said. He sounded like he was already working on the matter.

"Great," I said. "Oh, one more thing..."

"Your gun," he said, cutting me off. "Where do you want meet to get it?"

"Can't risk it. I don't know if I'm being watched." I told him where the truck was parked and suggested he swing by and put the gun under the driver's seat. Luckily, I had a spare key that was not taken when I was arrested. I hung up feeling a bit better knowing the plan was working...so far.

Chapter Four

Phillip Jacobs drove down Barrington Street headed for his office on Hollis Street. He had just finished placing Conway's gun in his truck as requested. As he drove, he was thinking about how he would cover Conway on his trip to Cape Breton, especially on the return run. It wouldn't be easy, he thought, since this whole operation was supposed to be secret. He knew there was corruption throughout the city and elsewhere; everyone looking to cash in on the illegal booze traffic. He, for one, thought Prohibition was a stupid idea but he was a cop, and he took an oath to uphold the law. But he didn't completely despair. He knew at least a half dozen or so men he could count on and one in particular.

Jacobs was originally from Barrie, Ontario. He enlisted in the Royal Northwest Mounted Police in 1919 shortly after his discharge from the army at the end of the last war. He served for four years in Regina dealing with smugglers along the Canada – US border in Saskatchewan. He was then re-assigned again, this time to his present posting in Nova Scotia to deal with the growing smuggling problem in the province.

He thought about Constable Marc Mombourquette up in the Sydney detachment. He was serving as a highway patrolman working with the local Provincial Police detachment, covering the whole of the northern section of Cape Breton Island. He and Jacobs served together back in 1921 for several months. He proved to be reliable, dedicated and a good friend. They posted him back to Cape Breton, his birthplace, upon hearing that his mother was gravely ill. If ever there was someone he could rely on, it was Marc Mombourquette.

"Constable Mombourquette," Marc said when he came on the line.

"Phil? How the hell are ya, my friend. What's it been two, three years?"

"A couple, yeah. How's your mother doing?"

"She died seven months ago.," he said.

"Jesus, sorry to hear that."

"Just as well. Things were not very good those last few weeks. Going when she did was a blessing. I heard you were posted to Halifax. So? What's up?"

"I need a favor."

"Sure thing," Mombourquette said.

"I can't go into details over the phone, but I can say I'm working on a very sensitive operation dealing with the smuggling of booze."

"Say no more. Whaddya need?"

Jacobs gave him a very brief rundown on what was about to go down in the Glace Bay area since he probably was aware of parts of the operation anyway. It was his beat after all, and he was a good cop.

"For now I need you to turn a blind eye to anything suspicious down that way in the next twenty-four hours."

"I see," he said.

"And you can't tell me more?"

"Sorry. This going to create a problem for you?"

"Not me personally but if word gets back to my sergeant..." He left the implication hang between them.

"Once my people get clear of your area, I'll square it with him if need be."

"When is all supposed to happen?"

"Sometime tomorrow according to my source."

"Right," he said. "I'll take care of it."

"Try and keep the number of people who know about this to a minimum if you can. The last thing we need here is for word of what we're up to getting out."

"Not a problem. I'm the only federal cop up here. There's also six local Provincial Constables, working in two man shifts, mostly in and around the populated areas. I do the outer areas."

"Jesus," Jacobs said. "Just how big is it?"

"Most of the northern half of the Island. Sound like a lot and it is geographically but most of the people live in the Sydney, Glace Bay area. There's an Indian reservation down around Whycocomagh which is close to Baddeck. So you're operation should be okay until it reaches the mainland. I assume it's heading back that way?"

"Yeah," was all Jacobs would say.

"Right. No more questions. Is there anything else you need?"

"No. And Marc...thanks."

"No problem. I hope you nail the bastards."

Jacobs hung up the phone thinking there was a good man.

* * *

We left Halifax by mid-afternoon. Our route was over to Dartmouth then out onto Highway Seven which took us to Sheet Harbour. We stopped for a short break and a quick bite to eat from the bag Lenny had packed with a half dozen meat sandwiches and a jug of hot coffee. We then continued on to Antigonish where we stopped for the last time for gas and to switch seats for the last leg which would take us through Baddeck and on up into the highlands.

During the trip I got to know a bit more about Lenny Purcell.

He was, as I thought when we met, a local fisherman working on a family boat out of Bear Cove about ten miles south of the city on the way to Sambro. Turns out his family, like so many during these tough economic times, turned away from fishing for a more lucrative payday in the rum running trade.

"So how come you're not on makin' runs with your boat?" I asked at one point.

"Too small to make the run that far out," he answered. "Plus, it don't have enough cargo space to make any money. 'Sides, me brother's running it now."

"Too bad. I reckon the money's better on that side of the business?"

"Yeah, sometimes. But I ain't doin' that bad. Besides, we don't hafta worry 'bout losin' our boat to the Customs patrols or hijackers."

"You said somethin' about that before we left. They a big problem?"

"Only lately," he said as he downshifted for a sharp turn. "Locals lookin' to cash in."

"You have any run in with them?" I asked.

"Once. Luckily, when they saw our guns, they took off. But they're gettin' more darin'. Won't be long afore someone gets hurt or shot dead."

"Jesus," I said.

"Amen to that. What about you? What's yer story?"

"Not much of a story to tell. I'm just another independent trucker tryin' ta make a livin'."

"Yeah, I get it. So how'd ya end up runnin' booze?"

"Buddy a mine put me onto it. Said if I wasn't too particular what I carried an' willin' to take a risk, he could set me up with a few quick runs. Luck ran out on my last one an' got stopped."

"Tough break," Purcell said.

"How it goes," I said, "Run with the devil ya gotta be prepared for a bite on the ass sometime."

"Ain't that the truth. Lucky for you ya met up with the Joudreys then."

"Maybe."

"Whaddya mean, maybe?"

"Let's wait an' see after this run if it was luck."

"Relax. The fella we work for has plenty a' pull so don't worry."

"Hey," I said, "one of the reasons I made my way this long is by a healthy dose of worryin'. By the way, where exactly are we goin'?"

I decided to stay away from anymore questions about who was running this operation for now. I felt like I was connecting with him and didn't want to put him on his guard.

"There's a cove jus' outside Glace Bay. We'll meet a boat there and take its cargo then head back to the city."

"Where's the boat comin' from? I thought all the offshore booze was down offa Lunenburg, Liverpool way?"

"Yeah, mostly. These guys are runnin' from the French islands offa Newfoundland. That's where the really good booze comes from."

"It's gonna be another long drive then?"

"A bit different," he said with a grin.

"Whaddya mean?"

"We ain't goin' back on the same road. We'll be headin' back to Port Hawkesbury through St. Peters on the southern road then, when we're back on the mainland, we'll head to Canso an' on back down the eastern shore an' home."

"Why we changin' the route?"

"The boss figures the best way to keep from gettin' caught by the government people and any hijackers was to mix up the roads we use."

"Good thinkin'," I said. "This fella sounds pretty smart?"

"Smart enough. I heard he went to school in England."

"No kiddin'?" Very interesting, I thought.

"I need ta take a piss. Shudna drank so much coffee."

"Yeah, no problem. Pull up over there." I pointed to a wide patch of shoulder up ahead.

He downshifted and eased the rig onto the gravel shoulder, making sure to not drop the front wheel over the edge of the shallow ditch beside the road.

"Thanks," he said.

We arrived in Glace Bay just after ten PM. It was a dark moonless night making the surrounding area hard to make out. There were not many streetlamps on this section of road. Shortly after we passed by the road into the town, Purcell pulled off onto a dirt side road.

"We're here," he said, slowing the truck and down shifting into second gear.

A few minutes later, I spotted the outline of an old wooden building sitting at the land end of a long wooden wharf.

He stopped the truck and turned off the engine. Opening his door, he looked at me and said, "Wait here."

I watched as he disappeared into the darkness. He re-emerged five minutes later and got back into the cab.

"Boat'll be here in about twenty minutes," he said. He must have met with someone inside that building, I reckoned.

"Can't be too soon for me."

"Gives us time to position the truck," he said starting the engine.

"Not a bad place for a drop off," I said. "Not much light though."

"Yeah. The local fishermen use it to unload their catch an' run it to the plant back in town. Some a' the loggin' people use it too. We'll have the lights on when the first boat comes in."

"So what's the plan when they get here?" I asked.

"You stay in the back an' see to it they load it right. Be sure to keep watch an' the count. Best way is lay the cases like this." He proceeded to outline the floor layout which would give the count we were looking for.

"Gotcha" I said.

"When we're done, I'll take ya over an' introduce ya to the captain since the next trip you'll be on yer own."

"Okay. We pick up in this spot all the time?"

"No," he said, shaking his head. "We mix it up. Accordin' to the boss, we don't wanna set up any, what he calls, patterns the CPS can figure out."

"Makes sense," I said.

He finally had the truck positioned where he wanted it. We got out and headed for the wooden wharf the jutted out into the cove. There was a wooden fish shack about twenty feet up from the end of the wharf with several wooden barrels and an assortment of fishing gear around it. I figured the leader of this operation must have made some sort of an arrangement with the owners to use the place.

I walked a little way toward the wharf. Four dories were tied alongside the wharf, two to a side. Each was manned by three men and were laden with equal loads covered by heavy tarps. I reckoned the cases of liquor were stacked beneath them.

Looking past them, I could just make out the silhouette of a two masted schooner out in the darkness. Unfortunately, I couldn't see its name. She wasn't showing any running lights nor were there any other lights lit on board. I thought I saw her darkened mainsail on the after half of the boat was still unfurled and hanging slack in the light wind.

My thoughts were interrupted when I heard Purcell whistle. He was waving for me to get ready to start loading. The dory men started transferring the cases to the truck. They worked quickly and without too much chatter. I couldn't make out what they were saying since it was in French.

We were down to the last twenty or thirty cases when Purcell called me over to where he and a man, I took to be the captain, stood watching the work. It turned out he was actually the Chief Mate. His name was Pierre Marcel Moulin. A Frenchman from Miquelon. We shook hands as Purcell introduced me.

He was tall and heavyset. I could see that he was strong looking despite the heavy woollen overcoat he was wearing. I reckoned him to be in his fifties, if the traces of white through his beard were any indication. He had a stern weathered face with deep set eyes under two thick eyebrows.

"Vingt caisses a faire," one of the Frenchmen loading the truck, called out.

"We're done here," Moulin said in near perfect English. He was holding out his hand.

Purcell pulled out a large envelope and placed in the man's huge, calloused hand.

"You gonna count it?" I asked.

He gave me a funny look then stuffed it in a pocket.

"No need," Purcell said. "We've been through this a coupla times already. Let's go. We got a long ride back."

With that we headed for the truck, and I got in on the driver's side.

"Which way? Back through the town?" I asked.

"Part way. I'll tell where to turn off. We're headin' back through St. Peters like I told ya then along to Port Hawkesbury. Here's a map. Follow the road I got lined out. We gotta try an' make the ferry by two o'clock if we wanna get back to the city on time. We're goin' back along the eastern shore."

"How many routes are there?"

"Three. You'll get ta know them easy enough. You, okay? 'Cause I'm gonna grab me forty winks before I take over."

"Yeah," I said, "go ahead. When do ya want me to wake ya?"

"When you reach Canso."

"Right."

I shifted into gear, eased the clutch out, shifted into first and headed for the road.

We switched up on the driving at Canso before we made it back to Halifax. We did it in good time and without any incidents, switching the man driving one more time. Once we reached the outskirts of the Township of Dartmouth, Purcell told me to pull over and we switched places for the last stage of the drive. Twenty-five minutes later he was wheeling the truck off the road and up a dirt track about a quarter mile before reaching the fishing village of Eastern Passage.

I was bone tired and hungry when we finally came to a stop beside a large, weathered barn at the end of the road. I spotted a black four door sedan parked on one side. He tapped the horn twice then he got out, telling me to stay in the truck.

"Back it inside when they open the doors," he said.

"Okay," I answered sliding across the seat.

A minute later two men appeared, pushing the big wooden barn doors open. I manoeuvred the truck around and slowly backed up inside. I spotted a third man inside in my side mirror. He was guiding me in. When he signalled me to stop, I stepped on the brake, turned the motor off and got out.

"Who da fuck is he?" the man who guided me in said as I walked to the back of the truck.

"New driver," Purcell said. "Jerome Conway."

"Yeah? Da boss cleared 'im?"

"What do ya think?"

Purcell looked at me and started to introduce the men who were now gathered at the rear of the truck.

"This fella 'ere is Bill Jollimore. Those two are brothers; Wayne an' Brian Hennigar," he said as he pointed to each one of the men. "You'll be dealin' with them from now on."

I nodded to the men, eyeing each one, committing their faces to memory.

"Right. Let's get this load off so we can get outta here," Jollimore said.

I untied the canvas flap covering the rear then climbed up into the box, tossing the flap up on top. One of the Hennigars climbed up as well.

I took a few seconds to look around. It was a typical wooden barn that had seen better years. The walls were filled with gaps and spaces between the boards but still solidly anchored to the earthen floor. There were a half dozen stalls along both sides of the room and a loft overhead. Six coal oil lanterns lit the area since there was no electricity. I notice a covered stack of cases sitting in one of the stalls.

"Let's get goin'," Purcell ordered. I wanna get back to town before sunup."

It took almost an hour to hand bomb the load from the truck to three of the empty stalls. When the last case was off-loaded, I pulled the flap back down and jumped off the back. It was then that I spotted the brothers moving several cases over to where I saw that smaller covered stack of cases.

I went over to where Jollimore and Purcell were standing looking over a couple of sheets of paper; probably the load manifest.

"If that's it I'll be off," I said, interrupting them. "How 'bout the rest of my money?"

"Yeah, sure," Purcell said. "Here."

He pulled an envelope out of his coat pocket and passed it to me.

"You did okay," he said. "We'll be in touch if you want more work."

"For this kind of payday, you bet," I said, stuffing the money in my pants pocket. "You got my number. Nice ridin' with ya."

"Yeah. You, too."

"Oh, ya need a lift back ta town?"

"No, I'm good," he said. "Bill will take me over. Thanks anyway. By the way, if yer ever lookin' for a good time, drop into the pig on Bishop Street. I'll stand ya a drink." He gave me the address.

"Right. I'm off."

I turned and headed for the front of the truck. When I stepped up on the running board I looked back and called out, "Can someone get the doors?"

Jollimore waved at Wayne Hennigar to go and open up. I started up and once the doors were open, drove away.

I paid particular attention to the area and made note of the significant landmarks leading back to the main road. I was curious about the location and how they set up their security to protect the liquor from local thieves. Then I remembered seeing one of the stalls was set up with a couple of cots and a small pot belly cast iron wood stove. I figured the Hennigar brothers were local lads hired to guard the barn. This was looking more and more like a well put together operation.

I arrived back in the city an hour later and parked the truck on the street near where I was staying. It was late and Mrs. Pottie had already turned in. I opted to turn in as well; it had been a long gruelling drive over some pretty rough sections of road, and I was bushed.

The next morning I awoke around eight-thirty. I got up, washed, and shaved then went to the kitchen where Mrs. Pottie stood at the wood burning stove stirring something in a large pot. When she heard me come into the room, she turned to look at me.

"Mornin'," she said with a pleasant smile. "You must've come in late. I didn't hear you."

"Yeah," I said. "I had a long run an' got back quite late. I don't suppose there's a chance of a mug a tea an' maybe some breakfast?"

"Sit ye down there." She pointed at the table. "I'll put a coupla eggs on, bacon okay?"

"Sounds good."

"I made some fresh bread yesterday. It's over there in the breadbox. Help yourself."

"Thanks."

I got up and went to the breadbox.

"I don't mean to pry, mind, but what is it you do?" she asked as she placed a mug of hot fresh tea on the table.

"I'm a teamster," I said, coming back with a thick slice of bread. "Mostly long haulin'."

"That why you was so late coming in?"

"Yeah. I had a round trip up to Cape Breton."

"That is a long way. That mean you'll be gone often?"

"Can't say. See, I own my own rig an' hire out when someone needs a truck to go outta town."

"Own your own truck, you say. Good for you. Best being your own man. My man's the same. He owns his own boat."

"Really? He must be away a lot. Where's he fish?"

"Mostly along the coast; the boat's big enough to make it out to the Banks but he don't go there often. Besides, there's just him and one other man to work the troll line."

She was referring to the fishing banks off Newfoundland and down off Yarmouth.

"I'm surprised he's still fishin'."

"Why wouldn't he? He's been fishin' since he was boy." She was just sliding the eggs and bacon onto a plate.

"I mean, from what I hear, the fishin' ain't been so profitable lately."

"We do alright," she said, putting the pate down in front of me. "We got no kids to see to an' we own the house, so we manage. He sells enough, an' what he don't sell we either keep or give to our church or trade with some of the neighbour merchants for goods like that bacon."

"Sounds like a good arrangement," I said, tearing off a piece of bread and dipped it into the yellow yolk.

"We've been here a while," she said this like it explained everything, which of course, it did.

I finished eating as she went back to her pot.

Later, I headed out. It was a nice day, so I opted to walk down to Lower Water Street. I needed to stretch my legs anyway after yesterday's drive. I also needed to find a telephone to call and check in with the boss.

I spotted a drugstore with a soda fountain counter inside and went inside. I asked if I could use their telephone which was mounted on the back wall. The clerk said it would cost a nickel, which I gave him.

"It's me," I said when Nancy answered. Her voice sounded great.

"Oh good," she said. "We were worried since your last call."

I picked up on the strain in her voice.

"What's up? Something happen?"

"Yes. But I shouldn't discuss this over the phone. Where are you?"

"About three blocks away."

"Good. You better get here as quick as you can."

"Right," I said, all business now. "Be there in ten minutes."

When I entered the office Nancy waved me straight through into McCarthy's office without a word.

Inside, I saw Phillip Jacobs and Matt Murphy sitting in front of him. They all looked at me as I closed the door and pulled up a chair.

"Glad you made it back," McCarthy said. "How did it go?"

"Pretty much as I expected," I said.

I proceeded to give them a detailed account of the events of the previous day, including the names of everyone I met.

"So the booze is being stashed in Eastern Passage?" Jacobs asked when I finished.

"Yeah, at least this last load is," I said.

"There're other locations?" Matt asked.

"Don't know, but from what I know already, I'd say the way this operation is set up it's definitely being run by a very smart operator. I think it'd be a mistake to underestimate him at this point. Oh, one more thing. Purcell let slip that whoever is runnin' things was educated in England, or so he's heard."

"Very interesting," McCarthy said. "That could help us narrow our search somewhat, don't you agree Phillip?"

"Maybe," Jacobs said. "There are a lot of people here with roots to England."

"True. But we must still consider this as an opportunity."

"Did you get the name of the boat, or the captain?" Jacobs asked, looking back at me, and bringing the conversation back to the matter at hand.

"No. It was lying out in the cove an' there was no moon. We dealt with the First Mate only; Marcel Moulin."

"And you say they delivered four hundred cases? Did you see what kind of liquor it was?"

"I got a glance at the manifest, yeah. Looks like it was mostly cognac and brandy."

"France," Murphy said, looking at McCarthy.

"Looks that way," he said, nodding. "Destined for the U.S. I should say."

"Most likely," Murphy agreed.

"Uh, Nancy, er, Miss Slaunwhite sounded like there's some sort of problem?" I asked, changing the subject.

"Yes," McCarthy said. "A situation came up while you were out of town. I will leave it to Mr. Murphy here to fill you in."

"Yes sir," Matt said, turning to look at me. "We had a bit of bad business late last night. That Boston gangster you reported, O'Leary, had a run in at one of the local speakeasies down on Bishop Street, resulting in one man killed and another in serious condition at the hospital."

"What the hell happened?" I asked.

"We're not sure. We're still putting the pieces together. You know what it's like: no one saw anything; no one knows anything. Usual crap. Near as we can figure out, this O'Leary went to this particular boozer and when he got there had a meeting with the owner, Lawrence Jenkins. Soon after, an argument ensued and that's when all hell broke loose."

"That's it?" I said when he stopped talking.

"That's it."

"And O'Leary?"

"In jail. We're holding him pending charges for capital murder."

I must have given him a quizzical look because he said, "We caught him with a pistol. The gun's being checked to see if it was the murder weapon. We're certain it is since there's evidence it had been recently fired."

"Where did you pick him up?"

"As it happened, there were two beat cops not for away when the shooting took place and responded within a matter of minutes. They caught him coming out with the gun still in his hand."

"Who'd he kill?" I asked.

"A man named Johnson. Kevin Johnson. We know about him. A local bootlegger runs a place up in the Fairview area. The other victim was just someone who drove him to the speakeasy. Probably one of Johnson's customers did the driving for free booze."

"So, what do ya reckon he was doin' there?"

"We've suspected for some time that one, maybe two, of the speakeasies are supplying a number of the bootleggers from their stock, most likely as a sideline for extra cash. However, for the life of me, I don't understand why a big-time hood like O'Leary would care if some speakeasy was pushin' booze out the backdoor, especially if that speakeasy has already paid for the booze? Makes no sense."

"Yeah," Jacob said, "we can't figure that part out yet. But I'd bet there has to be some connection to the over all operation."

"Possibly," I said. "There's gotta be somethin' that ties O'Leary, the bootlegger an' that particular place to each other."

I looked back at McCarthy who had been sitting there listening intently.

"So Jerome, any thoughts?" he asked.

Yeah," I said. "Remember I mentioned when we came back from the Cape Breton run and delivered it that place in the Passage? I told you that I also saw them shuffle a number of cases to a separate area. If I'm right, then they're skimming from the shipments comin' in and sellin' to the local market on the side. That would offer a plausible explanation where the speakeasy was gettin' booze to sell to the bootleggers, right?"

"Yeah," Jacob's said. "Pretty risky though, I mean stealing from the mob isn't the brightest thing to do...ever."

"True enough. But if that's what they're doin' an' the Yanks found out...?"

"Mother of God, you're right!" Murphy said.

"For one thing," I said. "We're into some seriously deep water here. When I was up in Cape Breton, I noticed that there are a lot of people in on this, and they look like they mean business. My impression is this operation goes beyond just local fishermen trying to make some extra easy money."

"Meaning?"

"Meaning there're a lot of guns and people who don't have a problem or any compunction about usin' them."

I noticed Matt Murphy nodding his agreement with my assessment.

"All the more reason we have to shut this down," McCarthy said. "Our problem is how do we proceed without endangering either our people or the general populace? This is not Chicago or New York, after all. We do not have gun fights on our streets. So? Suggestions?"

"Well maybe we could start by shutting down that Eastern Passage operation," Murphy said.

"I don't know," Phillip Jacobs said, looking from Murphy to McCarthy. "Sure, we could go after a significant load of contraband and maybe even target the illegal operators here in the city but that wouldn't stop the trade. It'd just drive it further underground?"

"Good point," McCarthy said.

"I agree with Phillip," I said. "Sorry Matt, but he's right. We'd only be causing nothing more than an inconvenience to those running the business and would likely spark even more violence."

"So what do we do?" Murphy asked.

"Stay with the original plan," I said. "Go for the one who's running the operation."

"Easier said than done," he said, morosely.

"Do not despair," McCarthy said, reaching for a folder on his desk. "This wire came in during the night. It is from Lee in Washington." He passed it across to me first.

"In it, Lee reports that through the extensive investigative apparatus of the Federal Bureau of Investigation, they have found a link in the chain that makes up the illegal distribution of liquor from here. It appears that they have unearthed information indicating that the man in charge here is a prominent businessman."

"We sort of assumed in had to be someone like that," I said, passing the file to Jacobs.

"True, but it could be anyone, making the field too hard to investigate without arousing suspicions or interference from certain areas. However, Jerome's little bit of information on this person's education could help shorten that list."

"Lee says that the FBI information suggests this man may have criminal connections in Montreal as well as in the States. That could be an avenue my people could look into." Jacobs said, passing the file to Murphy.

"A definite possibility," McCarthy said. "Proceed with that thought, but with care. Remember this is a closed operation."

"I think I can manage that," Jacobs said, then looking at Murphy, he added, "Maybe you can look at the local police reports and records. See if anything pops out."

"Yeah, I can do that," he said, placing the file back on the desk.

"Excellent," McCarthy said. "Good work everyone, especially you, Jerome. Let us meet again in twenty-four hours for a progress update. Jerome. Spare me a few more minutes, please."

The others stood and said their goodbyes, then left.

"This business with O'Leary is giving me a great deal of concern," McCarthy said as he sat back in his large leather chair.

"With good reason, I'd say," I said, thinking I had an idea where this was heading.

"Precisely. I do understand the limitations Constable Murphy is operating under in regard to gaining the confidence of the general public in this matter. However, it is imperative that we find out what occurred. To that end, do you think you can delve into this on your own? Without stepping on the toes of the local police or Constable Murphy?"

"Yes sir," I said. "I think I can get what you need, after all, I'm sort of working inside now. Besides, if I guess right, that speakeasy may be Purcell's waterin' hole which leads to me wonder what else it is. After all, it can't be a coincidence that he recommends the same place where O'Leary jus' happens to show up an' shoot someone, right?"

"Very astute observation," he said, nodding. "Very astute, indeed. Be very careful my boy. This is dangerous ground you are about to step on."

"Careful is my middle name, sir."

"Excellent. I will leave you to your devices and usual resourcefulness then. Keep in touch. If anything more comes in, Miss Slaunwhite will contact you. In light of the recent turn of events, I think it would be prudent to minimize your visits to this office. It would be best to avoid anyone seeing you. Therefore, I think it would be a good idea to have her pose as your lady friend. You agree?"

"Good idea," I said with a smile which caused him to raise an eyebrow.

"Quite so. That's all. Good luck."

I got up and headed out of the office.

Chapter Five

The next afternoon I headed for the speakeasy where the shooting happened.

It was located on Bishop Street in the basement of an old two-story stone house with a low-pitched wood roof. It was the fourth house up from Hollis Street. At the time I arrived there were several men hanging around the outside of the house, labourers, judging by their dress. As I neared them, they glanced in my direction, giving me wary looks.

"I hear a fella can get a drink hereabouts," I said, stopping in front of them.

"Yeah," one of them said after a moment. "Down the alley an' 'round back."

I nodded my thanks and headed down the alley. As I walked down, I was struck by the fact that they were open for business as usual so soon after a major crime took place. I knew many of these operators were connected politically at City Hall but even so, this was pretty goddamn fast. But that was Matt Murphy's problem, thankfully.

I found a door under a large four section window and thought I heard sounds of laughter coming from behind the door. I stepped up and rapped on the door.

A mountain of a man opened it and eyed me up and down. His bulk filled the door space. He had to be six foot and three hundred pounds of trouble.

"Yeah? Whaddya want?" he grunted.

"A drink," I said, taking an involuntary step back. "A mate said I could get one here an' maybe somethin' ta eat."

"Ya got money?"

I fished out a couple of ten-dollar banknotes and showed them to him."

"Good enough?"

He snorted and turned side on to me, indicating to me go come inside. Even from the side, it was a tight squeeze getting past him.

"Mind yer manners, 'ear," he said as I went down the half dozen steps to the finished basement.

The main room was laid out with plenty of tables and chairs, enough for about twenty to thirty people looking for a fun night out. There was a raised section of floor in one corner with an old upright piano against the wall. It was large enough for a small music combo to set up. A bar was built in against the back wall with a half dozen stools in front of it. I saw two long handles sticking up behind the middle section of the bar; obviously, the taps for the beer kegs tucked under the bar.

There were about a dozen or so people, men and women, sitting around the room and at the bar. Most were drinking glasses of beer. I had a feeling the women were 'working' girls getting an early start or hustling the customers to spend their money on drinks. I headed for an empty stool at the bar.

"Whaddya 'ave?" the barman said when he finally came over. He had been leaning on the bar at the other end talking with one of the men sitting there.

"Coffee," I said, turning side on to the bar, casually eyeing the room.

"Ya know this is a boozer," he said with a smirk on his face.

"Yeah, but I wanna coffee first, okay?"

"Sure, sure, don't git testy. Ya want milk an' sugar?"

"Jus' black. What's on fer sandwiches?"

"Got ham an' beef."

"Ham," I said, "with hot mustard. By the way, is that what it looks like?" I indicated a large ceramic jar a feet away.

"Yeah, made fresh dis mornin'. Twenty-five cents a dish."

It was not uncommon to find homemade Solomon Gundy in these places. It was a local pickled herring delicacy popular with the locals. I had to admit that I was partial to it myself.

"Sounds good," I said. "Gimme a double servin' an' bring a beer with the sandwich, thanks." I pulled out a dollar bill and slid it across the bar. "Keep the change."

"T'anks."

Just then I caught a glimpse of a woman getting up and walking my way. She must have spotted me pulling out my cash. A few moments later she eased up beside me and slipped onto the empty stool next to mine.

"Hiya honey," she said, trying to sound sultry, enticing. "Buy a lady a drink?"

I looked her over. She was in her early to mid-thirties, about five-four tall with ample breasts. Her dark blue frock has a slightly plunging front, exposing enough cleavage to pique a man's interest if he was looking. Her hair was dark brown and cut in the style of the time, wavy with bangs that reached to the top of her eyebrows. It framed her face nicely, making her appear younger than she was.

"Sure," I said. "Why not." I waved at the barman who was just about to bring my order and pointed at the woman. He nodded and reached under the bar. I knew he was reaching for a bottle of heavily watered-down liquor.

"My name's Sally," she said, smiling. "You?"

"Jerry," I said, pulling out another couple of dollars.

"New here?"

"Yeah, you could say that."

"Where are you from?"

"Around, you know."

"Yeah. So Jerry, whaddya do?"

"This an' that."

"Sounds mysterious," she said just as the barman arrived with everything. I slid the bills across to him and nodded. He swiped them up and walked away.

She picked up her watered-down drink that I paid full price for and took a sip.

"Mmm," she hummed, setting the glass down. "Nice."

I doubted it was nice at all, thinking these bar hustlers weren't being paid to drink.

"The place always this quiet?" I asked, looking around the room.

"No. You're early. You gotta be here after dark. That's when things get crazy."

"I heard there was some excitement here last night. Somebody got himself shot up?"

She gave me a funny look.

Uh-oh, I thought.

"Jus' curious, I mean, you say it gets kinna crazy. That sorta crazy I don't need."

She relaxed a bit at my explanation.

"That was jus' a fluke," she said. "Usually people jus' come here to drink and dance. Ya know, jus' to have fun."

"So? What happened?"

"Not sure. This swell came in an' I see him go into the back office. Then fifteen minutes later I hear three-gun shots. Next time I see him he's pushin' his way through the crowd, headin' for the door."

"Jesus," I said, feigning surprise.

"No kiddin'. I mean, I never seen anybody shot before."

"Then what happened?"

"The police arrived an' shut the place down. There were a lot of upset people I can tell you. A lotta them were swells from the south and west ends out for night of fun. Last thing they expected was for the police to take note of them, if get me."

"Yeah, I do," I said. "I'm surprised the place is open so soon."

"The owner's got an in at the city. Shame really that they shut the place down last night," she went on. "Everyone was jus' getting' into the swing of the night, you know, fun. Speakin' of which, you wanna have some fun?"

"Thanks," I said. "Not right now. Maybe later...if I come back. I jus' stopped in to check the place out an' get a coffee an' somethin' to eat."

"You sure ya ain't got time? It'd be worth it."

"I bet it would, but I can't. Sorry."

She signed, pushed her glass away and stood up. "Thanks for the drink. Maybe next time."

Not a chance, I thought, but said, "Sure thing, baby."

I watched as she went back to the table where was sitting when I came in. There was a man sitting there, smoking, and nursing a glass of beer. He gave me the hard eye from under his fedora which I ignored. I reckoned he was her pimp or partner.

I turned back to the dish of pickled herring, the barman arrived when I was about half-way through the plate of herring with my sandwich and a glass of beer.

"Jerry?" I heard someone called out behind me. I spun around and saw Lenny Purcell as he walked up and took the recently vacated stool.

"So ya decided to come by, eh?"

"Ya said I should come by an' give the place a try," I said.

"Hey, Frank," he called out to the barman. "Two beers. You gotta come by after dark," he said, turning back to me. "This is one of the better booze cans in town. Good music an' the booze ain't watered down too much."

"I take it ya come here often then?" I asked.

"More than other places, yeah. The boss has an exclusive deal with the guy owns the house."

"This boss you keep hinting at, he has a lot of operations?"

"A few. Mostly we supply the booze," Lenny said. It was then that I noticed he had a bit of a buzz on. Only reason I could think of why he would start talking about the business.

"Listen, whaddya doin' tonight?"

"Nothin' planned. Why? More work?"

"Naw. I was thinkin', why don't ya come back 'round nine an' you an' me spend some time getting' better acquainted. I mean, it looks like we're goin' ta be workin' together, right?"

"Sounds good," I said. "Sure. Why not."

"Thing is though," he said, putting a hand on my shoulder. "Ya gotta wear a suit an' tie. After the sun goes down is when the swells come out."

"Yeah, okay. I can manage that."

"Okay." He picked up his glass and gulped down half the contents in a single swallow then set it on the bar.

"Gotta go," he said, standing up. "See ya later."

"Yeah, see ya later."

I watched him walk to the door at the back of the room marked, 'PRIVATE'. This was turning out to be an unexpected break for me. It looked like I was about to get my foot much further in the door of this operation a lot quicker than I expected.

He came back ten minutes later looking worried.

"What's up?" I asked when stood next to me. "You look like someone jus' walked over your grave."

"Don't even say that in fun," he said, signalling Frank over. "A double, an' quick."

"Jesus man, what happened?"

"You hear anythin' 'bout a shootin' in here last night?"

"Yeah. I heard some people talkin', why?"

"Never mind 'bout any of that," he said, picking up the shot glass that Frank just placed in front of him and downing most of the liquor in a single swallow. This brought on a spat of coughing as the raw liquor hit the back of his throat. I patted him on the back, but he waved me off.

"Look," he said at last, "'bout tonight. We gotta do it another time. Somethin's come up. I gotta go. Me or someone will get in touch, okay?"

"Yeah, sure," I said. I waited for him to tell me something more, but he didn't. He picked up the shot glass and finished off the little that still in it and hurried out.

I had a feeling whatever rattled him had something to do with what happened here last night. It didn't look like I was going to get any more information so I decided to try and find Matt Murphy to see if he could shed any more light on the situation. I was about to finish off the beer Lenny dropped on me when I saw a man approaching.

"You a friend of Lenny?" he asked as he sat on the stool vacated a moment ago by the self-same Lenny.

"Maybe," I said, feigning an air of suspicion. "Who's askin'?"

"Don't be testy. I was jus' curious. I thought I knew most a' his mates. Name's Pete," he said. offering his hand. "Pete Surrette. You?"

"Jerome Conway," I said, taking his hand.

"Well, Jerry. Whaddya do?" He chose to call me by the more familiar form of my name.

"Trucker. Long distance haulin'," I said, giving him a wary look. He sounded like a hustler thinking he just found an easy mark.

"No kiddin'. Now ain't that a coincidence."

"Yeah? How so?"

"Well, ya see, it's like this. I got a bit a work if you're interested." He leaned in closer.

"What sorta work?"

"The kind that pays pretty good to the right fella who's willin' to not ask too many questions, if ya get me."

"Yeah, I get ya. What makes ya think I'm one a them guys?" I was still playing it cool with him.

"Well, you an' Lenny for one thing," he said.

"What's that got to do with anythin'?"

"I know him an' what he's inta."

"An' what else?"

"Huh? Whaddya mean?"

"Ya said for one thing, what else makes ya think I'd be interested?"

"Nothin' else," he said. "It was jus' a figure of speech. Jesus."

"Forget it. I'm jus' messin' with you. So? What 're you offerin'?"

"I need somethin' picked up an' delivered back here to my place."

"What an' where?"

"How big is your rig?"

"Deuce and a half."

"That'll do. It's a hundred cases of booze. It's down in French Village. You know where that is?"

"I can find it. How soon ya need it an' how much ya payin'?"

I'd like to have it here by tomorrow night. What do ya need to make the run?"

"A hundred an' fifty plus gas. Half up front. The rest when I deliver."

"That's a bit steep ain't it?"

"Ya want the booze or not? Take it or leave it."

"Okay. Ya gotta a deal. When can you leave?"

"Soon as you hand me the money and give me the particulars. By the way, how come ya thought ya could trust me?"

"Lenny said you were okay."

"So you an' Lenny were talkin' ' bout me then?"

"He's my cousin an' we do some business off an' on, ya know, on the side from his usual business."

"His boss know what he's doin'?"

Surrette gave me a funny look.

"Jus' wanna know in case he doesn't and takes exception to him moonlightin' is all. I don't need any grief in my life."

"Yeah, sure, I get it," he said, seemingly satisfied with my answer. "So? Ya still interested?"

I realized I had an opportunity here to nail another link in the smuggling chain and one that just fell into my lap.

"Why not," I said. "I can always use the money."

"Good. Let's get outta here."

He slipped off the stool and headed for the exit with me close behind. Once out on the street, he led me over to where his car, an older model four door T-Ford, was parked.

"Get in," he said. I went around to the passenger's side and got in.

He started the car and eased away from the curb.

"Where we goin'?" I asked.

"My place," he said. "You want your money, right? Well, I don't go around carrying that kind a cash in my pocket. I'll also give you the particulars on where you'll make the pickup. Anything else?"

"Yeah," I said. "What kind of trouble can I expect?"

"The road is patrolled by one Mountie, usually durin' the day. Most a the time he's at his detachment office, so you shouldn't have any problem there."

"Good. What about hijackers or the locals tryin' to take the load?"

"There's a risk of that, of course. There are a coupla families down that way who've tried to hijack one of my shipments in the past, but I managed to beat 'em off."

"They armed?"

He shot me a quick side long glance.

"Sometimes, why, that change anythin'?" he said.

"Jus' so ya know, if there's any gunplay, I want an extra hundred if I get back with the load. You okay with that?"

"Yeah okay, I can handle that," Surrette said as he turned the car into a driveway beside a large house. We were down in the south end of the city close to where the city's rail yards were located.

We got out and went inside. He led me into a well-appointed parlour and, after pouring out two glasses of whisky, laid out everything I needed to know. Then he gave me half the money I asked for. He went to the door and pulled on a cloth sash hanging from the ceiling. A moment later a heavyset man came in. He wore a lose fitting two-piece suit.

"You come by tomorrow 'round two. Douglas here will go with you as a ride along, he knows where to take you," he said. "Good luck. I'll wait for you at the drop off point with the rest of your money."

"Right," I said. I put the money in my jacket pocket and followed Douglas out to the car. He had orders to take me where I wanted to go.

I decided to head for a little cafe I found downtown. We drove in silence. I was no sooner out of the car when he spun it around and drove off. I flipped him a salute with a flick of my finger against the brim of my hat.

Chapter Six

I arrived back at the house on Atlantic Street at quarter of two the next day. I got out and was half-way to the front when it opened, and Douglas stepped out. He wore working clothes today which seemed to suit him more than dressy clothes he wore last night. He definitely looked more comfortable.

"Ready?" I asked when reached me.

"Let's go," he said, moving by me toward the truck.

Once we were out of the city, I kept an eye open for a gas stop. I spotted one that was open and pulled in.

"I gotta gas up an' take a leak," I said, shutting the engine off and opening the door.

"Okay," he muttered.

"Wanna soft drink or anythin'?"

"Naw, I'm good."

I met the attendant as he came out from the small one bay garage. I asked him to fill me up and if he had a phone. He did. It was inside the garage's office. I glanced back at the cab. Douglas looked like he was napping. I went in and dialed Phillip Jacobs' number. He picked up on the second ring.

"Constable Jacobs," he said.

"Phillip, it's me, Conway," I said.

"What's up? You have something?"

"Look, I don't have much time. Do you know anything about someone named Pete Surrette?"

"Surrette, you say," he said. "Yeah, we know the name, why?"

I filled him in very quickly on the situation and gave him as much as I had so far.

"You live under a lucky star, my lad. And this just fell into your lap?"

"More or less," I said. "I went to the speakeasy where O'Leary was arrested to see if I could find out what happened. That's when Lenny Purcell came in. He'd been drinking and was a little talkative so I thought I might get something outta him. But he went inside the owner's office and when he came out said he had to leave. He looked worried. I thought about following him but decided against it. That's when Surrette approached me with this job."

"So what's your plan? You want me to send our man down to…?"

"Christ, no. This might be an opportunity to find out where the booze came from and who is running it from the mother ship."

"Okay," he said. "It's your play. I'll handle it anyway you want. I'll pass this information on to McCarthy though."

"That's okay, but for now, let me see what else I can find out after I get there."

"Right. Watch your back. We've heard report that there's been some activity down that way involving guns."

"Anyone hurt?" I asked.

"Not yet, but the way things are going it probably won't be long before some yahoo takes a shot at someone."

"Gotcha, thanks. I'll call in when I get back." I hung up just as the gas jockey came in, wiping his hands on an oily rag.

"Goin' far?"

"Liverpool," I said.

"That's a long run. I see yer runnin' empty?"

"Doin' a pick-up. Whadda I owe ya?"

"That'll be two-fifty for the gas plus ten cents for the call," he said, stepping behind the short counter.

"Thanks," I said, passing him three single bills. "Maybe I'll see ya on my return run."

"Ain't goin' anywhere, so most likely ya will."

I went to the truck, got in. Douglas was definitely in dreamland. I headed back onto the road.

It was just past eight o'clock when I turned down the road leading to French Village.

"Hey," I called out to Douglas. "Wake up."

"Wha...?" he grunted as he opened his eyes.

"We're on the road to French Village. Time for you to tell me where ta go."

"Yeah, sure," he said, sitting up and rubbing his eyes. He looked out the windows to get his bearings. "Right. 'Bout a mile down da road you'll see a side road on da right. Take it," he said.

"Okay," I said.

I drove on, keeping my speed around twenty miles an hour. It was not long before we neared the side road.

"There, Douglas said, pointing. "Turn up there an' keep goin' 'til ya see a blue fish shack on da left. Should be a boat tied up there. Drop me off an' then look for a place to turn 'round. Park by the shack an' git ready to load up."

"Gotcha," I said.

Once I was positioned at the shack, I got out and went to the rear of the truck. Two more men were already there, one untying the canvas flap.

"Dis 'ere is Ernie Boudreau. Da other guy is Willy," Douglas said by way of introductions. The men looked like the typical fishermen you find up and down the coast.

I climbed up into the storage area in back of the truck.

"One a' you guys get up here an' lend a hand," I said. Willy was the first to move. Minutes later, Ernie and Douglas started carrying cases out of the shack and setting them on the tailgate, where Willy and I started moving them up near the front.

It took a little over twenty minutes to load all the cases. When everything was counted, I threw a tarpaulin sheet over the cases then jumped down. Boudreau closed the shack up and rejoined Douglas at the back of the truck.

"Boss sez he'll let ya know when the next shipment comes in," Douglas said, passing a wad of money to Boudreau.

"We'll be waitin'. T'anks," the old fisherman said, stuffing the money into a pocket of his weathered overalls.

Douglas and I got in the truck and made ready to head off.

"Seem like good folk," I said just before we reached the main road. I slowed down to make the turn.

"Yeah," he said. It was clear I would not get anything more out of him, so I just concentrated on driving.

The trouble came a half hour after I left French Village in the form of four men standing across the road; two armed with rifles. I saw a one-ton truck parked on the side of the road which I reckoned they planned to use to haul the load away.

"Whaddya wanna do?" I asked Douglas.

He reached inside his coat and pulled out a pistol.

I pulled out my forty-five, chambered a round and clicked the safety off then rolled my window down.

One of the unarmed men stepped out from the others and started to wave me down. I shifted into a higher gear and floored the gas pedal. I put my gun out the window frame and fired two rapid shots into their truck, making sure not to hit anyone. It had the desired effect.

The four men scattered off the road as I sped past them aiming my gun in their general direction and shaking my head. At least one of them saw me. I hoped he got the message. As I neared a turn in the road, I glanced in my side view mirror to see if they were going to follow me. It didn't look like they were. Guess they weren't expecting someone to shoot at them. Worked for me.

I didn't ease off the gas for the next mile, wanting to put as much distance between them and me as I could. I figured they must've been alerted to my load and set up the ambush. That could only mean one person...Boudreau. He must've set the hijack up after Surrette alerted him that I was coming down. Of course, it could be just as likely that since it was a small village, word could've got around about the booze and the locals set the thing up themselves. Either way, it was Surrette's problem, at least until Phillip Jacob's shut him down.

I had to admit, this set up Surrette was running piqued my curiosity. It seemed to me to be pretty small in terms of volume he was dealing in. And where was he getting the liquor from? Again, the volume was not worth the risk. There had to be something more going on between Surrette and Purcell and that speakeasy where I met Surrette. By the time I reached the gas stop I filled up at earlier I decided I would have to take a closer look at these connections, circumstantial as they seemed.

I pulled into the gas pump and got out. The same man came out and ambled toward me.

"I'm goin' to check in an' let your boss know we're back," I said to Douglas who sat hunched in the corner of the cab.

"Okay," he muttered.

"Back agin, eh?" the gas attendant said as he approached the truck. "More gas?"

"Yeah," I said, stretching, "an' I need to use the phone again."

"Go ahead. Ya know where it is."

I made two calls: one to Surrette and the other to Jacob. I got Surrette on the second ring. He gave me an address up in Rockingham and said Douglas knew the way and he'd meet us there. I told him about the run in with the hijackers but said nothing happened, so he didn't owe me any more than my other half of the agreed price for the run. I couldn't reach Jacob. I would have to call him tomorrow.

I settled up for the gas and phone calls then hit the road again.

Surrette and another man were standing beside his Packard when we got to the rendezvous. I eased to a stop about twenty feet away and shut the engine off. I wasn't sure what would transpire out here away from any witnesses and I definitely didn't know these men enough to trust them, so I put my pistol in my coat pocket where I could get it if needed. I got out and stepped toward them.

"Glad you made it," Surrette said. He was wearing an overcoat with a thick fur collar. I recognized the other man as the one who drove me to my truck before I left. He wore an overcoat as well, however, not as expensive as his boss' one. It was unbuttoned and he had his hands stuffed in the coat pockets. I was pretty sure he had a gun in one of them.

"Yeah," I said, looking back at Surrette. "Where you want to unload the goods?"

"See that building over there?" There was a small barn like building about fifty feet away.

"Right. I'll back up to the door. Have your man here open the doors. By the way, is he gonna help me unload?"

"No. There're two men inside waiting."

'Uh-oh,' I thought. But went and moved the truck. He followed in his car.

As it turned out, I had nothing to worry about. The unloading went smoothly and quickly. When the unloading was finished, I walked over to him.

"Job done. My money?" I asked, holding out my hand.

"Of course," he said, taking out his wallet and extracting a number of banknotes. "There's an extra fifty dollars for a good job. I might have more work if you're interested?"

I took the money and counted it before putting it in my pocket.

"We'll see," I said.

"Well, if you want more work, you can always find me at the speakeasy. If I'm not there leave word with the barman, Frank, or let Lenny know."

"Gotcha. Now if ya don't mind I gotta get me some sleep."

Later, when I got back to my room at Mrs. Pottie's, I took out a lined notebook that I had secreted inside a false bottom of my carryall. I used it to keep a record of my findings and activities. I went over the events of the day from my arriving at the speakeasy to my return from French Village.

Three questions stood out in my mind. One: Why was Lenny Purcell at the speakeasy and what was his contact with the owner about, and what was behind the way he acted after the meeting with him? Two:

Pete Surrette. Why did he single me out to approach to hire for a liquor run? Was it more than a coincidence? Three: Did these two events suggest that there was a connection between Purcell, Surrette, and the speakeasy? Then there was the matter of the O'Leary shooting. Was it connected? The more I considered these and other questions the more I felt there was more going on than it seemed.

I checked the clock on the nightstand; it was close to one in the morning. I decided it was time for a meeting with McCarthy and the others.

The next morning I called in. Nancy picked up.

"CPS. Mr. McCarthy's office." The sound of her voice brought back happy memories.

"Hi," I said. "I'm coming in. Let the old man know and get in touch with Jacobs and Murphy. I'll be there at ten, okay?'

"Sure thing," she said. "Has something happened? Are you okay?"

"Yes, and yes. By the way, if it's possible, I'd like to see you tonight if you haven't got anything else on?"

"I don't, and I'd like that."

"Hoped you'd say that. See you at ten." I hung up and walked back to my room with a big grin on my face.

"Somebody's happy this mornin'," Mrs. Pottie said as I passed the kitchen door.

"Looks like someone's got himself a date maybe?'

"Maybe," I said. "If it works out, I'll be late in."

"No problem, dearie. I'll leave the porch light on. You have fun." She turned away with a giggle.

"Thanks. I will."

I went back to the room and collected my notes for the meeting then ten minutes later, headed out. I decided to walk since it was a decent day and the morning air felt fresh and clean from a soft northerly wind off the Basin.

I arrived at the office building at the same time as Matt Murphy and we entered together. I knew I was taking a bit of a chance coming here during the day but what I had to report was important and the others, especially Jacobs, had to know about it.

"Must be important," Murphy said, giving me a sidelong glance. "I mean, you coming in during the day."

"You must be a mind reader," I said.

"Huh? What do you mean?"

"Nothing, forget it. Yeah, it is important. But let's wait 'til we're all together, okay?"

"Sure."

I headed up to McCarthy's floor. When I reached it, Murphy followed behind as I walked straight for the meeting room where we first met. I stopped long enough to poke my head in McCarthy's office to let Nancy know we were here and where we'd be.

"Okay," she said. "Coffee?"

"Yeah, thanks," I said.

Once everyone was in attendance, I related the events of the last twelve hours including my thoughts on the double-dealings that appeared to going on and how the O'Leary shooting might be connected.

"You've been very busy," Murphy said when I finished.

"I agree," Jacobs added. "Not bad for a few days on the case. Walter here was right when he said you were good."

"Thanks," I said.

"With everything you collected so far we could put a real dent into their operations," he went on to say.

"Maybe, but I think we have a good chance of finding the ringleaders, which is the main objective of this campaign," McCarthy stated.

"Think we might be getting a bit too ambitious," Murphy said. "I mean, consider what we have so far; a secret cache over in Eastern Passage, a ship's name running liquor from Miquolon, a second operator working here in the city. Not to forget, O'Leary; a known criminal in the Boston underworld."

"Everything you say is true," McCarthy said. "However, all these things and people can be replaced and rebuilt. The brains behind the setup is who we need to bring down. He is the one who has orchestrated everything and who has all the connections. It is him and his network I want."

"Yes sir. I meant no disrespect."

"None taken. I do understand your position, particularly as a policeman, but when you take down a bad tree, you must also dig out its roots. Now then," he said' looking at me. "What do you propose next?"

"I think Purcell made an error when he allowed me to see the skimming operation," I said. "I think I can use that to get in deeper. I plan to work my way into his confidence enough for him to bring me to his boss."

"And you think he'll go for it?" Jacobs asked.

"Don't see why not. After all, I've proven myself and he did expose his cache to me. So if I let him know I want in..."

"But only if he takes you to his boss."

I just smiled.

"Well, gentlemen, I think that concludes our business for now. We push on."

The meeting was over and as everyone filed out of the meeting room I hung back and stopped at McCarthy's office after he went inside.

"Are we still good for tonight?" I asked Nancy with a smile.

"What've got in mind?" she asked, smiling back.

"Dinner and then..." I shrugged.

"Tell you what. How about the 'and then' first then dinner."

"I always liked to have an appetizer before the main course."

"How about both being the main course?"

"You're on. Eight?"

"I'm feeling hungry. Seven."

I blew her a kiss then left.

* * *

Allister Fenwick paced over the thick Persian rug; his hands, balled fists, were pushed deep inside the pockets of his smoking jacket. He was angry. And afraid. He did not like to feel these emotions which only compounded his displeasure.

"My God," he said, his voice sounding strained. "What possessed the man to do such a thing?"

Tony Caruso sat in one of the thickly upholstered wing-back chairs; a cigarette in one hand, a crystal glass of whisky in the other. He had one leg crossed over the other.

"Had to be done," he said. "They had to be given a lesson."

"But..." Fenwick started to say, stopping, and looking at him. He took his hands out of his pockets and raised his arms.

"No' buts'. These people gotta learn there's a price to pay if you try an' steal from us."

"I understand that, but couldn't he have gone about it differently? I mean, shooting someone. Really! This will create problems. Problems I may not be able to control. How in the name of God did they catch him?"

"Cops must have been nearby, they showed up just as he was leaving the speakeasy. Unfortunately, he hadn't time to get rid of the run before they nabbed him."

"Damn it all. I do not need this on top of the last seizure. It will draw too much attention to us and the operation."

"You worry too much. There're ways to handle this."

"Perhaps in New York or Chicago but this is Halifax."

"So?"

"So. What he did just does not happen here. This is a seaport with a strong military presence. Serious crimes like murder simply do not happen here. Handling one when it does occur, especially a murder, will bring in the police and possibly even the RCMP."

"So what," Caruso said, taking a sip of his drink. "Cops is cops. We know how to handle them."

"You still don't understand. This is not the States. The police here do not operate the same way."

"You sayin' they ain't dirty?"

"No. They are just as corruptible as police anywhere, I suppose. But the main difference is this is an English town with very strong connections to British traditions."

"Yeah? So what?"

"You do not understand. When I say this is an English town, I mean everything about it is connected and influenced by the English from its business community to the government."

"So?"

"So. That means every aspect of life here is different than what you are accustomed to back in Chicago. For example, the local villains do not carry guns here."

"Yeah," Caruso said. "I wondered 'bout that."

"The only ones carrying weapons are the police," Fenwick went on. "And the laws are very strict when it comes to guns."

"Okay, so no one carries a gun, what's that gotta do with dealin' with the cops?"

"Corruption exists here as it does everywhere. You just have to know how to take advantage of those, um, opportunities."

"You're sayin' we buy off..."

"Yes," Fenwick said, cutting him off with a wave of his hand. "But it must be done discreetly and with finesse. Fortunately, I have spent enough time and money cultivating the right contacts to cover our operations."

"Then use them to find out whatever they got on our business before we lose anymore product. Got it?"

"Yes, 'I got it' as you put it."

"Good. Now what's the story on this next shipment?"

"I have ordered another delivery from our friends in Miquolon. It should be on route as we speak."

"You're not usin' the same routes, are you? Won't the customs patrols be watchin'?"

"No, they are not sailing on the same route, or using the same boat, for that matter. This time I am using one I have an interest in. The shipment will be transferred to a waiting boat that will bring it to Jeddore. Once loaded on the truck, it will be taken to Mahone Bay where it will then be re-loaded into a coastal steamer and delivered to the final destination in Maine as you have instructed."

"When is the shipment due to arrive?"

"Late tomorrow night."

"Sounds good," Caruso said. "Let's hope it works out as good as it sounds. In the meantime, what're you goin' to do about O'Leary?"

"I'm not sure there is much I can do," Fenwick said, a hint of nervousness creeping into his voice.

"Not good enough. You sold us on the idea you were some hot shot here, so do whatever it is we're paying you to do an' get him out."

"Look. I know what I told your people but that did not include you lot coming here and murdering someone. The liquor business is easy compared to this. I am not sure how far my influence goes when it comes to the Crown Attorney or the Justice Minister."

"That's not my problem. Jus' do something to get him released; I'll do the rest once he's outta jail."

He finished his drink, set his glass on the end table beside his chair and stood up.

"You got twenty-four hours."

He turned and walked out of the room. Moments later he was outside and heading for the waiting car at the curb.

Fenwick stood at the bay window and watched through the embroidered curtain as Caruso climbed into a black Packard that was parked at the curb. He was considering the current situation he now faced. Fenwick was beginning to realize that things were escalating out of his control and threatening to potentially expose him to legal jeopardy. Perhaps the time had come for him to consider a return to England, or perhaps the Continent, Portugal maybe.

'Why not?', he thought, still looking out at the now empty street. He had enough money to live very comfortably for a long time, particularly after he sold off his business interests and real estate holdings here in Canada. He saw a hint of a smile on his face reflected in the windowpane. He turned away thinking there were several calls he had to make.

Chapter Seven

I was back at my digs sitting at the small wooden writing table that made up part of the furnishings making the latest entry in my journal. My thoughts were interrupted by the sound of someone out in the hall.

Mrs. Pottie rapped softly on my door.

"Jerome?" she said as she pressed her ear against the door. "Are you awake?" Hearing nothing, she rapped again, this time a little louder.

"Huh?" I grunted, looking up from the journal and automatically closing it. "Yes? What is it?"

"Sorry to disturb you but there's a man on the phone wants to talk to you. He sez it's important."

Pushing the chair back, I stood up, glancing at the clock on the nightstand: the dial read twenty to eleven.

"Okay. Thanks, I'll be down in a few minutes," I called out.

I put the journal back in its hiding place and quickly pulled a clean shirt. I poured out a glass of water from the ewer on the nightstand and took a deep drink and headed for the phone, hoping it wasn't McCarthy or worse, Purcell.

"Hello," I said, leaning close to the mouthpiece and picking up the receiver, holding it against my ear.

"Jerry," Purcell said in my ear. Damn my luck.

"Whaddya want Lenny?"

"Jesus, you always this cranky?"

"Whaddya want?" I said again.

"Got a job if yer interested."

"When?"

"Tomorrow. It's a big one this time. A full load. It'd be worth two hundred. Whaddya say?"

"Sure, why not."

"Great. Meet me at the boozer where we were the other night, say in a coupla hours? I'll fill ya in then."

"Yeah, okay," I said.

"Right. See ya then." He hung up and the line went dead.

I placed the receiver back on the hook on the side of the phone and headed back to my room to get ready for the day.

I could hear Mrs. Pottie at her usual place in the kitchen. The scent of frying eggs and bacon wafted up and my belly stirred in an anticipation.

"You sure have been lucky," she said as she set a plate in front of me. I had already poured a cup of tea when I came into the kitchen.

"How so?" I asked.

"Well, since you moved in you're hardly ever here; always away someplace. I didn't know there was so much work 'round for truckers?"

"Yeah, it's been busy. But that won't last. Never does," I said. "This time next week I could be scrapin' for just a quick run cross town."

"That bad?"

"Sometimes, yeah. Right now, there's a lot of work for some reason. I don't ask bein' happy to makin' some good dosh so I can put some aside for the hard days."

"You're a smart one. More tea?"

"Thanks," I said, holding out my mug. "Whaddya mean 'smart'?"

"You ain't squanderin' your money like some I know."

"Don't see the point. Besides, I ain't much of a drinker an' it's too risky to play around the boozers."

"Like I said...smart."

"Thanks."

"Will you be in for supper tonight?" she asked, stepping back to the stove with the teapot.

"Dunno. Best you don't plan on it. I'll grab a bite outside."

"Alright. You have a good day an' be careful."

There are moments when I think she thinks of me like a mother would.

I stopped at the phone in the hall on the way back to my room and called the office.

The sound of Nancy's voice evoked some very pleasant memories of the preceding night, bringing a broad smile to my face.

"Mr. McCarthy's office," she said.

"Hi," I said. "How're doin' this morning?"

"You know full well how I'm doing." She had lowered her voice almost to a whisper. I could hear the happiness in her voice.

"Want an encore performance?"

"Anytime. Is this a social call then?"

"Not really. I need to talk to the boss."

"Okay, just a moment," she said, then added, "tonight?"

"You're on."

"Anytime lover," a brief pause then, "he's ready for you."

Something had changed between us lately. Something that felt great. I realized I was feeling happy about where this seemed to be going and was happy about the prospect.

"McCarthy."

"It's me," I said.

"So soon. Has there been another development?"

"Purcell called me this morning. Looks like there's another job and he said it's a big one this time. A full load."

"Excellent. When and where is this to take place?"

"Don't know yet. I'm meeting him this afternoon. Only thing I have so far is the job takes place tomorrow."

"I see. And is it still your intention to proceed with your plan to try and infiltrate deeper into their organization?"

"Yeah. They slipped up when they let me see their little sideline over in the Passage, and then that run for Surrette, which presents too good an opportunity to get closer to the top people."

"Do you think they will go for it?"

"I'll find out on this run. If Purcell skims any of the product and we take it over to their hiding place again, that's when I'll approach him."

"You realize that you may very well be exposing yourself. What if he doesn't go for it? Would that not put you at some risk?"

"Every time I jump in that truck, I'm putting myself at risk," I said.

"Good point," McCarthy said. "I will leave it to your good judgment and hope for the best. Do you want me to alert the others?"

"Not yet. Maybe later when I have more information. I'll try and check in after I meet with Purcell."

"Right. Be careful and good luck." The line went dead.

* * *

A couple of hours later, I was sitting at a small table in the corner of the speakeasy nursing a cup of coffee. I was smoking a Black Cat cigarette, my third since arriving twenty minutes ago. Lenny was late.

I was feeling a bit keyed up like I usually felt before going on a job and his being late wasn't helping my nerves. So many things could go wrong if I didn't play my cards just right. So much depended on what the job entailed and whether he would try and skim the load again. The plan depended on it. My problem was when to brace him with my offer to throw in on their operation. The upside would be putting me in touch with whoever was running the operation...maybe. The downside, simple, kill me and just take the truck. I instinctively put my hand inside my coat and felt for my .45, feeling reassured as I wrapped my hand around the grip.

About five minutes later, I spotted Purcell as he entered the room. He stopped for a moment, scanning the room then, seeing me, stepped quickly towards where I sat. He pulled out chair and sat down as he waved at the man behind the bar, pointed at my mug then held up one finger. The barman nodded.

"You're late," I said, feigning a tone of impatience.

"Not that much," he said. "What's it matter to you anyway?"

I shot him an angry look as I reached for the ashtray and butted out the cigarette.

"So? What's the deal this time?" I asked.

"Remember that last shipment the CPS nabbed? The one that put the Joudreys in Rockhead?"

"Yeah, so?"

"So, this is the replacement shipment."

"We're headin' for Cape Breton again, then?"

"Not this time. We're pickin' it up in Jeddore over on the Eastern Shore. Then we run it to that warehouse in Eastern Passage we were at last time. We'll stay there until nighttime then we run it down to Mahone Bay, where we off-load to a tramp steamer that'll be waitin' there for us."

"I didn't know there was a dock big enough for a ship down there?"

"There's ain't," he said. "The Joudreys'll be there to help with the transfer. By the way, we gotta be there and done before sun up. That gonna be a problem?"

"Not for me," I said. "Depends on how fast we get unloaded. I can make the run in about three, four hours from the Passage. It seems like a lotta work this time. Why not jus' transfer the load directly to the tramper outside the twelve-mile limit or in the Bay?"

"Don't know. That's the way the boss wants it done, so that's the way we do it."

"I seem to recall Bill Joudrey tellin' me that there's a CPS patrol boat operatin' down that way. Ain't we takin' a risk of gettin' caught?"

"That's been dealt with," he said.

Interesting, I thought. Did they have someone inside the CPS?

Just then the barman arrived carrying a mug of coffee and set it in front of Purcell.

"Da boss called. Wants ta talk to ya," he said, looking at Purcell.

"Right," Lenny said. "He say when?"

"No," the man said, shaking his head. He turned and walked off.

"Problem?" I asked.

Don't know," he said. "Might jus' be some new instructions." He pulled out a watch from his vest pocket and glanced at the time. "I'll call him in a few minutes an' find out."

I decided to implement my plan now. "I gotta question for ya," I said.

"Shoot."

"I wanna say first off, I appreciate the work an' the dosh ya been puttin' my way."

"No sweat. It's workin' out for both of us."

"Yeah, but I got a bit of a worry."

"Yeah? What?"

"Well, I figure you or your boss is runnin' some sorta side operation that's maybe connected with Surrette. Mind you, I don't care what you fellas are up to, but if you are up to somethin' an' if anythin' goes sideways, it's my ass on the line, see what I'm sayin'? I don't mind takin' a risk of jail time if the money's good, or even risk gettin' shot at, but if I'm goin' to do that then I want to make worth my while, understand?"

"Go on," he said a bit warily.

"Well, the money's been good so far, but I figure I gotta chance of maybe makin' more. So I want in."

"Or what?"

"Or nothin'," I said with a shrug. "We keep goin' like we been doin', except I get a bit more money. After all, ya been runnin' my rig pretty hard these last few days an' upkeep ain't cheap."

"I get it, but it ain't up to me."

"Okay, who then?"

"Look, all I can do is talk to the boss, okay?" he said, ducking my question, not that I expected him to give me a name.

"Yeah, okay, but don't take too long. So, where we headed again?"

"Jeddore. A small fishin' village 'bout forty miles or so outside the city. The CPS patrols are light down that way."

"The boat can come in?"

"Close enough," he said. "There's a coupla fishermen down there that'll run the load from there to us."

"Hope they also got some extra hands to move the goods," I said, "or we'll there all night."

"Don't worry 'bout that. We should be on the way back in about two hours."

"How far is it?"

"A coupla hours each way. We'll head out tomorrow 'round noon. Meantime, get some rest, it's gonna a long day. Pick me up here at eleven in the mornin'. We'll cross over on the ferry and head out from the Dartmouth side.

"You said somethin' 'bout goin' back to the Passage an' havin' to stay the night."

"Yeah. This time we'll hole up at the storage barn with the load until we head out for Mahone Bay later the next day. Why? You gotta someplace ya gotta be or somethin'?"

"No, jus' curious is all."

Okay. I gotta go an' call the boss. See ya tomorrow at eleven." He got up and headed for the door at the other end of the bar.

I left ten minutes later and made my way back to my digs. I stopped at a drugstore that had a payphone and called in to McCarthy.

"Hi, good news," I said when Nancy answered the call.

"Let me guess," she said.

"Yep. But first I need you to let the boss know somethin', he in?"

"Not at the moment. He's having a business lunch with the Justice Minister. If it's important I can reach him. They're eating at the Halifax Club."

"No, that's okay. Jus' tell him the pick up is goin' to take place at a place called Jeddore over on the Dartmouth side. Then we're layin' over in the Passage before headin' to Mahone Bay. We'll be hookin' up with the Joudreys, who'll be runnin' the load out another ship."

"That's it?"

"Tell him, I'll try and get the name of the boat to pass on to John Lee in Washington. Also, let him know that I made my opening move. He'll know I mean."

"Alright," she said.

"So, about later. What say I take you out for dinner?"

"What do you have in mind?"

"I'll let you know that after dinner, but for now, you pick the place."

"Oh you," she said, chuckling. "Pick me up at seven."

"See ya at seven." I hung up the phone, smiling from ear to ear thinking about the night ahead.

I walked down to the front parlour. Mrs. Pottie was sitting in her favourite chair; a wooden rocker; she was mending a pair of work pants, presumably her husband's.

"Afternoon'" I said, stepping into the room.

"Jerome," she answered.

"I wanted to let you know I probably won't be in tomorrow night. Another job."

"Like I said before, you have been busy since coming to town, haven't you?"

"Yeah. I got lucky and made a good contact with lots of work."

"Well, good for you," she said as she slowly rocked back and forth. "I hope you're puttin' that money into the bank like you said earlier, you know for a rainy day or maybe..."

She gave me a sly look, her eyes twinkling.

"Uh, yeah, I am," I said warily.

"Don't you go worryin' none, now. I haven't been pokin' my nose where it shouldn't be. These eyes been around a long time. I remember when me an' my ol' man were young an' frisky. Heh, heh."

I could not help grinning as she said this.

"Been married long?" I asked.

"Goin' on twenty-five years," she said.

"Any children?"

"Had a son. He's gone now."

"Gone?"

"The sea took him. Six years back. A gale came up an' his dory capsized. They couldn't get to him in time."

"Jesus," I said. "I'm so sorry to hear that."

"Thanks. But we're okay. That's the life of a fisherman an' I still got my man."

"I been meanin' to ask, when will he be home, I'd like to meet him?"

"Maybe in few more days, dependin' on the catch. So, where you off to this time?" she asked, changing the subject.

"Down the Eastern Shore then back to town. I'm staying overnight. I don't like drivin' at night over a road I'm not familiar with."

"Sensible," she said. "Will you be in for dinner tonight? There's a chicken in the oven."

"No, I'm eatin' out tonight and won't be back until late."

"Alone?" she asked, looking at me from under her eyebrows.

I just smiled.

"Well, I better get freshened up. Is there enough hot water for me to take a bath?"

"Yes, the tank's full. Have fun."

I turned and headed for my room to get ready for my date with Nancy thinking Mrs. Pottie was one cagey old woman.

* * *

Lenny Purcell got out of the taxi and stood on the sidewalk outside Allister Fenwick's stately house.

It was a red brick two story structure set about forty feet back from the sidewalk and fronted by an expansive sod lawn. There was a low hedge along the bottom and two trees on either side of the flagstone walkway leading to the double doors; each with etched glass panels in the upper half. The house was not the most prominent or expensive on Young Avenue, but no one would ever think anyone but a swell lived here. If any doubted that, all they needed to see was the 1920 Bentley parked beside the house.

He went to the door and rang the bell. A moment later the door opened, and he was greeted by Edward, Fenwick's valet and sometime butler.

"Mr. Purcell," he said in his formal voice as usual as he took a short step back. "You are expected. Please follow me to the parlour. Mr. Fenwick will attend to you in a few moments."

He followed Edward into the well-appointed parlour.

"I have been instructed to offer you a refreshment."

"Huh, oh, no... thanks, I'm good," he said, taking the chair he usually sat in when he had to come here.

"Very good," Edward said then turned and walked out, leaving him alone.

Several minutes later, he heard footsteps in the hall then watched as Fenwick stepped into the room.

"Lenny," he said, eyeing him as he went and sat down in a thickly padded Wingback chair. "Your call sounded urgent. Has something gone wrong?"

"No sir," Lenny said, leaning forward. "Everythin's set for tomorrow. We'll be headin' away 'round noon an' then back to the Passage by dark."

"When are you heading for Mahone Bay?"

"Early evenin' the next day. The boat's not due to arrive until eight or nine o'clock I'm told. I already called the Joudrey's. They'll be there waiting."

"Excellent," Fenwick said. "So why this visit?"

It's the new guy, Conway."

"The man who owns the truck?"

"Yeah. He's done pretty good the last coupla runs. Seems to know the lay of things pretty good. Smart fella too."

"So?"

"He sorta figured out the game you're runnin' with the booze."

"Yes and?"

"Like I said, he's smart. He wants in."

"We are paying him enough for his time and use of the truck, aren't we?"

"He isn't complainin' about what we're payin', he jus' figures he could do better if he joined up for a cut of the action."

"What do you think? Can we trust him?"

"Well, he sorta knows a lot already an' is still willin' to run the loads. I don't see the harm. Besides, if he becomes a problem..."

"Quite so. I will leave the matter in your hands. Just keep his cut reasonable, say ten dollars a case. That will give him more than what you have been paying so far, I think. But no more, understand. And he is to understand that he will be working for me exclusively."

"Got it. There's one more thing. He wants to know who you are."

"Really? Why?" Fenwick asked.

"Sez, if he's gonna risk potential prison or gettin' shot, he wants to know who he's doin' it for."

"Too bad. The answer is no. You are only one locally who knows of my involvement and that is the way it will remain. If he does not like that, too bad."

"Yes sir," Lenny said, standing up. "I'll take care of it."

"Call me after the ship to Maine has been loaded and is underway."

"Yes sir."

Back outside on the sidewalk, it was still early, and the weather was pleasant enough, so he decided to walk down to the bar for a drink and maybe a visit with Mable, one of the girls working there as a 'hostess' for a bit of fun.

* * *

It was at the same moment, in another part of the city that I was sitting opposite Nancy in the dining room of the Waverley Inn on Barrington Street. She looked beautiful in a black dress with a bright red silk scarf tied loosely around her neck. She was not one for excessive make-up but what she did use she wore to great effect. She still had her cloche with a button shaped like a flower on the side. One of the things I liked best about her was her decision to not follow some the

151

current fashion trends many single women opted for these days.

"Having fun?" I asked. We had just finished our main course: halibut steaks with a medley of vegetables and were ending with slices of freshly made blueberry pie and coffee.

"Mmmmm," she hummed with a satisfied smile.

"Guess that means you won't need anything' else,"

She put her hand over mine and gently squeezed it, saying suggestively, "Don't bet on it."

I raised my hand, signalling for the waitress.

"Cheque, please."

Chapter Eight

Lenny and I were sitting in the cab of truck parked in the middle of the open deck of the ferry as it crossed over to Dartmouth; we were on our way to Jeddore.

"'Bout that matter we discussed yesterday, ya know, 'bout you throwin' in with us."

"Yeah?" I said.

"I told the boss an' he's okay with it. I sorta stood up for ya, tellin' him you was reliable and did good on the last coupla runs. He's agreed to let ya in. How's ten bucks a case and the same for any barrels ya carry sound?"

"Ten dollars a case, you say, an' only on the loads I carry?"

"Well, most a the time you'll be carrying at least a coupla hundred cases. You do the arithmetic."

"Hell, that's two hundred per load same as what you're payin' me now, but that'll be okay. An' who pays the gas?"

"You do but think about it. You'll be carrying everythin' we move. That's the other part of the deal; you'll be workin' exclusively for him now. Mind you, most of the loads won't be this big, usually around a hundred and fifty to two hundred cases at a time plus any barrels."

"Okay. Say I'm interested. When do I meet the head man?"

"You don't. That ain't part of the deal. No one but me an' a coupla others know who he is an' he wants to keep it that way. Take the deal or leave it; your choice."

Damn, I thought, there goes my one good chance to learn the identity of this man.

"I'll take it," I said.

"Good, welcome aboard. There's a coupla things ya hafta know. First, you're never to go to the Passage hideout unless he sends ya, clear?"

"Clear," I said. "What else?"

"Our biggest customer is a gang down in Chicago. Part of Capone's organization. Sometimes they send people up here, so ya might run into them, but don't worry, you still work for us, not them."

I didn't let on I'd already met Caruso.

"Was that fella what did the shooting the other night one of them?"

"Yeah, 'cept he's from Boston. We sell to an Irish gang runnin' the trade down there. Mostly, though, our main business is with the Italians."

"Christ, you guys run with some dangerous company."

"You got that right an' don't you forget it. They ain't a forgivin' bunch if you screw up, but that's why the money's so good. Looks like we're here," he said as the ferry neared her mooring spot.

I turned the engine over and waited for the deckhand to wave us ahead.

It was a long and tedious drive from Dartmouth to Jeddore over mostly passable roadways, at least until we passed Musquodoboit Harbour, then we hit a rough section.

"You been down this way before?" I asked, veering away from a sizable pothole. "Is the rest a' the way this bad?"

"Yeah," Lenny said, bracing himself against the dashboard. "Don't remember it bein' this bad though."

"Jeddore that good a drop off location?"

"The boss has a deal with some a' the locals. Why?"

"Jus' wonderin' is all," I said. "I mean, I'm in, right? I figure I might as well get to know what's what."

"Yeah, well, you'll get to know what need to know as we go."

'Uh-oh', I thought. Got to be careful and not press too hard. Questions in the wrong place and time could blow my cover, or worse, get me killed.

"Yeah, okay. Sorry."

"Forget it. See that side road comin' up on the right? Turn in there. Then we go about a quarter mile. You'll see a dock 'bout a hundred feet or so past it. That's where we pick up the load."

"Right. Is there a place to turn around? I don't want to back up that road in the dark."

"Yeah, you'll be okay. There's plenty a room. The local fishermen use the place to load their lobster pots. By the way, when we get there, you'll see two a' those fishin' boats. They're workin' for us so don't get nervous."

"Right."

It was just gone seven o'clock when I finally had the truck positioned to take on the load. The two boats Lenny had mentioned cast off and started for the open water once they saw us. It was too dark to make out the names of the boats or get a good enough description of any of the men on board.

"This could be tricky," I said when I stood beside Lenny at the rear of the truck.

"How so?" he asked.

"The dark. How're we 'spose to see anythin'?"

"Not a problem. The boats got lights rigged up on board."

"Oh. How long is the run in from out there?" I tilted my head, indicating the distant and unseen horizon.

"Dependin' on how fast the ship can sling the load, about half an hour each load. The two boats can usually run up to four hundred cases in a coupla hours if the water behaves."

"Good. That means we should make it back to the Passage around one or two in the morning."

"Yeah, that's what I reckoned as well."

"I hope we don't lose too much of the liquor on the return run," I said, glancing back at the roadway.

"It'll be okay," he said, following my gaze. "The cases are packed with hay to prevent breakage on the crossin' from Miquolon."

After several quiet moments, I said, "A while back when we first met you said you're a fisherman."

"Yeah. Man an' boy. My ole man had his own boat. We fished outta Sambro. Why?"

"Nothin'. Jus' wonderin', ya know, why this? I mean, fishin' is dangerous enough but rum runnin'?"

"Family had to eat an' there was still the bills to pay."

"Be harder to do from a prison cell, I'd a thought."

"Yeah, maybe so, but the money proved too good to pass up an' besides, the fishin' wasn't paying what it used to."

We went quiet for a moment or longer. "Well, this prohibition crap can't last forever. Maybe you can get back to fishin' when it's over," I said.

"If I do, it'll be on my own boat, or maybe a coupla boats. How 'bout you? You seem to be a smart fella. Why you doin' this?"

"Same's you. The money. I'm stashin' my money an' maybe one day I'll open a small truckin' company with a coupla trucks."

"Hm. Jus' a coupla big dreamers, eh?"

"Ain't no harm in dreamin'," I said, taking out my pack of cigarettes and offering him one, thinking I liked this man and would have been happy to be friends under other circumstances. "Trick is to keep yourself free an' loose to cash them in."

"Ain't that the truth of it. Thanks," he said, pulling one out. I lit a match and cupped my hands around the flame as we both lit up. Part of me felt bad knowing that when this assignment ended, I would have to arrest him which meant sending him to prison. But that was the hand he dealt himself.

We didn't have to wait long before spotting the outline of the first boat pushing its way through the water, its after deck laden with cases of liquor stacked five high and six deep, thirty cases a trip. It was obvious it was loaded to its capacity from how low in the water it ran.

"Right," Lenny said as he headed to the wharf to tie it up when it came alongside. "See if you can roll down a bit more; it'll help speed up the transfer."

I got back into the truck and, using the side mirrors, I slowly eased the truck back another ten feet. I stopped because it was too dark to clearly see where I was steering, and I did not want to put too much weight on that wharf. I got out and went to the rear of the truck where everyone was already hand bombing the cases onto the truck. I climbed up and helped Lenny lay them out over the floor. I noticed at one point that one of the fishermen was giving me an odd look.

We finished loading the liquor two hours later. It was definitely a full load. I was just finishing tying down the tarp over the rear of the truck when I spotted Lenny down on the wharf talking with one of the fishermen. He was handing them a fistful of money as the man stole a glance up in my direction. I wondered what that meant.

Eventually, we made back onto the main road and were heading back for the Passage. Lenny was at the wheel, wanting to take the first hour or so. I didn't mind. I was bushed from the drive down, the loading, and the exertions of the previous night at Nancy's place.

Soon after we switched seats, Lenny asked, "You ever do any work down this way before?"

"No, why?" I answered, keeping an eye on the black unmarked road.

"Jus' that ole Charlie back there thinks he's seen you some time back."

"Nope. Wasn't me. Where's he 'spose to've seen me?"

"Didn't say, jus' that you seemed familiar to him is all."

"Don't know what to tell ya, mate. I only arrived here a month back lookin' to make some dosh."

"From where?"

"Ontario, mostly. But it got too hot for truckers up there, what with all the illegal traffic between Canada an' the U.S. Besides, I wasn't too crazy 'bout gettin' involved with the Yankee mobs on my own, especially the ones outta Chicago. Too goddamn dangerous. Speakin' of which, what's the story with that O'Leary fella?"

"You don't need to know 'bout him an' Caruso. They're the boss' problem."

"Fair enough," I said. I wanted to try and change the subject away from questions about me. I heard the alarm bell ring in my head the second Lenny asked me if I ever worked down this part of the province. Funny thing was, I had no recollection of ever dealing with the fisherman named Charlie. I would need to be even more careful from this point on.

We arrived at the Eastern Passage location around one-forty, a good half hour ahead of schedule. Lenny instructed me to pull up to the door of the barn. He got out and went to the rear and unlocked the doors then swung them open. He went inside and turned on the lights before he came out and signalled for me to back the truck inside.

"We'll leave the truck here until tonight. Shut down and' come with me," he said.

"Why we gotta wait so long?" I asked, stepping down from the cab. "Wouldn't travelling durin' the day be simpler?"

"Simpler maybe but there'd be too many chances of runnin' into a curious copper. 'Sides, the ship won't arrive until tonight."

"Oh. So where do we hole up?"

"We'll stay at Bill Jollimore's place. You met him on that first run from Cape Breton. Now c'mon an' give me a hand. Open the back."

He went and pulled the doors shut while I untied the flaps at the back of the truck. I took a look around the large open space. There were two piles of stacked cases covered with tarpaulins against one of the walls. I reckoned there were fifty cases all together. Must be product they were skimming from previous loads. These guys were definitely playing a dangerous game here. If the Americans ever caught on to what they were up to...

"Okay," Lenny said when he rejoined me. "Let's get this off."

"How many you takin'? I asked.

"Twenty cases. Put 'em over there." He pointed to a space next to the two stacks.

We finished moving the cases and I retied the tarp over the rear of the truck. We left the building and after Lenny locked the doors, led the way across an open field.

"Jollimore's place is jus' on the other side of the hill."

Fifteen minutes later, we were sitting at a kitchen table with Bill Jollimore drinking glasses of rum; his wife was at the stove frying up a meal of corned beef hash. I had to admit it smelled good, the aroma made me aware that we hadn't eaten since leaving Jeddore.

"So what's the plan for tomorrow?" I asked.

"We hole up here til dark then we head out like I already told you," he said, lifting his glass.

"Yeah, I got that part. What I'm askin' is what're we doin' for the day?"

"Don't know 'bout you fellas," Jollimore said. "But I'll be out on the water. Still gotta catch us some fish."

"Sounds good," Lenny said, setting the glass back down. "If you don't mind, I'll go out with ya."

"Yeah, sure. Always good ta 'ave extra hands on board. How 'bout you? Wanna come along?"

"Me? Hell, the only thing I know 'bout fish is how to cook it," I said. Making the two men break out into a laugh.

"Okay," Jollimore said. "Ya kin stay back an' 'elp my woman."

I stole a quick glance at his wife, who had turned and was looking at us. She looked to be in her late forties, maybe early fifties. Her hair was still dark brown and thick. She stood around five-five and had a slender figure with small breasts. But it was her face that drew the eye. It was like so many women living this life, but hers still retained enough of the beauty she once had in her youth. She caught me looking at her and gave me a quick smile. I sensed there was a bit of mischief behind it.

"Well, if I'm goin' fishin', I best get some sleep," Lenny said. "Four AM comes early."

"You know the way to the bedroom," Jollimore said. "You kin bunk down there as well, Dere's two bunks." He nodded at me.

We finished our drinks and the plates of hash and fresh bread his wife set in front of us then got up and headed to the bedrooms.

I awoke the next morning to sunlight streaming in through the partially drawn curtains and shining on my face. I took a quick glance at the old wind-up alarm clock on the washstand next to the bed: seven-fifteen. Looking over my shoulder, I saw that Lenny's bunk was empty and remembered he said he was going fishing with Jollimore.

I rolled out from under a thick handmade quilt, sitting on the edge of the deep mattress. I got up, stretched, listening to my joints popping in little snaps. Shaking off the early morning chill, I got dressed before heading to the privy down the hall to wash up.

I walked into the kitchen fifteen minutes later to find Jollimore's wife standing at the sink, washing dishes.

"Mornin'", I said as she turned slightly and glanced over her shoulder at me.

"Mornin'. Breakfast?" she said, looking at me.

"Sure. Thanks. Mind if I help myself to a mug of that coffee I smell on the stove?"

"Mugs are in that cupboard there. Help yerself." She pointed to a cupboard on the wall beside the wood burning stove.

I opened the wooden door and took out a heavy mug. I picked up a hand towel that was draped over the back of a chair and reached for the cast iron pot sitting at the back of the stove.

"You want some eggs an' toast?"

"Sounds good, Thanks."

"Kippers?"

"Yeah, sure," I said, pulling out a chair at the table and sitting down. "How long ya reckon Bill an' Lenny'll be out there?"

"Should be back 'round noon, maybe mid-afternoon. Depends on the fish."

"I see. You got anythin' needs doin' around here? I'm glad to help out."

"Eat first," she said as she cracked the eggs into the cast iron pan beside a filet of fish. "Bill left a coupla chores for ya to work on."

"Great," I said. I thought I would try and learn more. "How long you been livin' 'round here?"

"It's my home," she said, picking up the pan and sliding the contents onto a plate. "Been down these parts all my life. Same with Bill."

"Must be tough livin' in such a remote area?"

"Ain't too bad. Lots a family around."

"Got any kids?"

"A boy. David." She turned around and set the plate in front of me. "Toast'll be ready in a minute."

She opened another cupboard and took out a can of condensed milk and a dish with a block of oleo on it, setting everything on the table.

"He take up fishin' as well?"

"No. He's a pretty smart fella. He got some education an' went to the city. Got himself a good payin' steady job there workin' at one a' them places that make things."

"Lucky him," I said, then dug into the meal.

I spent the better part of the day doing odd jobs around their property: chopping wood, stacking fishing gear. Lenny and Bill Jollimore came back about midday. They were coming up the path from the dock area. Bill had a small bucket with some fish in it;

guess I knew what was on the menu for supper.

Lenny and I were back on the road just after sundown. I drove most of the way down to Mahone Bay, switching off with him when we reached the outskirts of the town.

"We gotta a bit of a wait when we get there," he said. "The boat's gonna be late be a coupla hours."

I did not ask how he came to know that, figuring he got word somehow back Jollimore's place.

"Okay."

He drove the truck along a dirt road on one side of the Bay that eventually took us to a spot with a couple of wooden wharves built out from the shore. I spotted a boat that looked familiar tied alongside one of them. It was the Joudrey's boat. I saw Bill and Ken standing on the wharf talking to a couple of men. Lenny tooted the horn to let them know we were coming.

"Hey, Jerry," Bill called out when I stepped down from the cab. "Good ta see ya again."

"Yeah," I said as I walked to the four men. "You, too. Hi Ken."

"Jerry." he said with a nod.

"Who're yer friends?" I asked.

"Pete and Sam," he said.

"Fellas," I said. They simply nodded their acknowledgement.

"Right," Lenny said, looking at Ken. "Let's get started with the transfer. This is a big load this time."

"When's the ship due?" Ken asked.

I started to untie the tarp flap.

"'Round eleven. We'll load ya up an' then ya head on out in the bay an' wait."

"Lucky it's a calm night," Ken said, looking out over the water. "No wind."

"I thought the ship was comin' in an' we were to load it directly?"

"Change a' plans," Lenny said. "Let's go."

It took us over an hour to transfer all the cases of booze to the Joudrey's motor launch and secure it for the run to the steamer. Lenny paid the two men who helped us then came back to the boat.

"Tell the captain we lost a few cases on the run from Jeddore. I'll let the boss know when we get back." he said to Ken. "Good luck."

"Thanks," Ken said. "Do us a favour an' cast off them lines will ya?"

We went to the cleats on the wharf that the boat's lines were tied to and let them go. I watched and waved as Ken manoeuvred his boat clear, thinking that I wouldn't be able to get the ship's name to pass on to McCarthy.

"Okay," Lenny said. "If you're ready let's get outta here. You drive. Drop me off at the speakeasy when we get back to the city."

It was almost one in the morning when I dropped him off. Lucky for him, these places run until at least four most nights. For me, I headed to my parking spot where I have been leaving the truck then walked back to the Pottie's place and my bed.

Chapter Nine

I awoke at seven the next morning and got up. After a hearty breakfast of sausages and eggs that Mrs. Pottie made for me, I took my second mug of coffee and went back to my room. No one would be in the office yet, since it was only ten past eight. They usually did not arrive much before eight-thirty. This gave me time to update my journal. I kept a record of my findings on every case I was assigned in the event I had to give testimony at trial. I finished at eight-forty-five then went and called in.

"Mr. McCarthy's office," Nancy said, the sound of her voice bringing a smile to my face.

"Hi baby," I said.

"Hi, yourself. Where are you?"

"In my room, why?"

"Just curious." I detected a hint of playfulness in her tone.

"Now, now. Behave."

"You're no fun," she said. I could imagine the cute pout she would always have on her face when she was being playful.

"Wanna bet?"

"When?"

"Tonight...maybe. In the meantime, let the boss know I'm comin' in. Oh, an' see if you can reach the others an' see if they're available."

"Okay." She was all business now. "What time?"

Noon. I'll be comin' in through the back door, so let the guards know."

"Right. See you when you get here."

I hung up the phone and went back to my room.

* * *

Everyone was sitting in the meeting room when I arrived at the Customs Building, including Nancy, who sat next to McCarthy, notebook open and ready. We exchanged quick smiles.

"Ah," McCarthy said when I stepped into the room, closing the door behind me. "You're here finally."

"Hi, everyone," I said as I took a seat at the table.

"What's the latest?" Phillip Jacobs asked.

"I pulled out my journal and proceeded to give them a detailed rundown on the last thirty-six hours.

"You've been busy," Phillip said when I finished.

"You could say that," I said. "I'm puttin' in for a vacation when this business is done."

"And it will be gladly given," McCarthy said. "You certainly have earned one. However, we still have work to do. Are we any closer to identifying the ringleaders?"

The three of shook our heads.

"There might be a way," I said.

"Go on," McCarthy said.

"Purcell. As near as I can determine, he checks in every day, or at least is in touch with whoever it is. That being so, maybe Matt or Phillip here can put a tail on him; see where he goes. But, if you do," I said, looking at them. "You got to make sure they know what they're doin'. It's my butt on the line if they blow it."

"Not to worry," Phillip said. "I got just the man for a job like this."

"Good," I said, then looking back to McCarty, "unfortunately, I wasn't able to identify the steamer. The best we can do is to let Lee know the approximate time an' location where she sailed from. Maybe his people can work out somethin'. You can tell him it was a big shipment, over three hundred cases and some barrels, probably filled with rum."

"Miss Slaunwhite will attend to that immediately after we are done here. Is there anything else?"

"I have been hearing rumours on the street that people are worried about the news of the killing a couple of nights ago. There has been talk about gangsters running around the speakeasies and other drinking places," Matt Murphy said, speaking for the first time.

"That was to be expected," McCarthy said. "How does that bear on this business?"

"Not sure, but I know some of the people involved in the city and they won't hesitate to arm themselves."

"That is exactly what we must avoid. What is the latest in regard to O'Leary?"

"He is still being held in Rockhead with no bail pending a trial date. However, I have learned that a lawyer was in to see him."

"I see. Do you know who this lawyer is?"

"Christopher Winslow."

"Winslow...Winslow. Why does that name sound familiar?"

"He's been the legal council for a number of people we have arrested in connection with the illegal sale of liquor," Matt said.

"Ah, yes, now I recall. It might be instructive to find out who has been retaining him."

"I'll look into it."

"Good. I may make a call or two as well. Now, if that is all..." he said, looking around the table.

When no one said anything, we all stood, and Matt and Phillip filed out of the room. I hung back.

"Can you spare a moment?" I asked McCarthy when he walked past me.

"Certainly," he said. "My office. Five minutes. Miss Slaunwhite, come. You have a call to make."

I was sitting in front of his desk when he came in and joined me.

"Something on your mind that couldn't be shared with the others?" he asked.

"On two separate occasions, the last being on this last job, I raised the possibility of the CPS catching onto us and Purcell let slip that the cutters operatin' in the areas we were workin' had been 'taken care of'. I didn't press him for details for the obvious reasons, but what he said does raise the question of someone inside CPS being on their payroll."

'That would be a concern," he said, sitting back in his thick leather-bound chair. "There is always the possibility that someone in our organization could be bought. They are only human after all. And you say that he has alluded to this twice?"

"Yes sir. First time was when we were up in Cape Breton then again yesterday. The only area I can think of that would be able to give information on the cutters' movements or, for that matter, redirect them away from where he's operatin', would be the coastal radio stations."

"Good point. Thank you for bringing this to my attention and doing so in private. Anything more?"

"One more item. When we were down in Jeddore, one of the local fishermen that was helping us with the load, might have recognized me. I don't know from when or where."

"And did you know him?"

"No. I have absolutely no recollection of the man."

"So, why do think he might have recognized you?"

"On the drive back to the Passage, Purcell asked if I ever worked down Jeddore way before."

"I see. What do you want to do?"

"Keep goin', of course. But I jus' wanted to let you know that I might be compromised and that we might have to take action without finding out who's running the show."

"Well, let's press on while we can. I will leave this to you to handle as you see fit."

"Yes sir," I said as I stood up and headed for the door.

Phillip was standing in front of Nancy's desk looking over some papers she apparently gave him when I emerged from McCarthy's office. She was on the phone speaking with someone, most likely the long distance operator.

"Good," I said, "you're still here."

"What's up?" he said, looking over his shoulder at me.

"I need a favour." I stepped over by a row of filing cabinets against the opposite wall.

"What do you need?"

"One of the fishermen who helped us with the load in Jeddore was a guy named Charlie."

"Yeah, so?"

"I think he somehow might know who I am which means who I also work for."

"You sure about that?"

"No. For the life a me I have no recollection of the man. What I want from you is to have one of your men down that way nose around and try an' find out who this guy is."

"Okay," Phillip said. "Then what?"

"Arrest him."

"On what charge?"

"I don't care. Jus' isolate him, at least 'til this business is done."

"I'll see what I can do. What else can you tell me about this Charlie?"

"Not much," I said. I gave him all I remembered about his description and his boat.

"By the way, do you know where Lenny Purcell lives?"

"Sorry," I said with a shrug. "You can likely find him at a speakeasy down on Bishop Street. Seems to be his favourite place. It might also be connected to his boss."

"Okay, thanks. Let's keep in touch directly from here on in. Here's my direct number."

He pulled out a small notepad and jotted down a phone number which I then committed to memory.

"Thanks, will do."

We stepped back to Nancy's desk. He dropped the papers she had given him on the desk and then said goodbye. Nancy was still on the phone. From what I heard, she had to be talking to John Lee. She finished the call a few minutes later.

"Done," she said, looking up at me with a smile and her big beautiful brown eyes.

"So... tonight?" I said, sitting on the corner of her desk.

"Okay, but I was thinking. How about I cook us dinner?"

"And she can cook too," I said, chuckling.

"I have many talents...and a few secrets."

"So I am learnin'. What time?"

"Seven, okay? We can eat around seven-thirty."

"Works for me. See you then. Can I bring along anything?"

"Just your, um, appetites."

* * *

Allister Fenwick stood rigidly beside the small table, looking down at the candlestick telephone. It was ringing. He had a very good idea who was on the other end and didn't want to talk to that person. On the sixth ring he reached out and picked up the phone by its long neck and lifted the receiver off, putting it to his ear.

"Hello?" he said into the mouthpiece he held close to his face.

"It's me," Caruso said. "What's the latest on gettin' O'Leary out?"

"I have managed to secure legal council for him. He has agreed to take the case and has gone to the prison to talk with O'Leary."

"That it? Nothin' else?"

"These matters take time. You're not in the States now. The system here is completely different as I have tried to explain to you."

"I don't give a shit 'bout that. You only need to get him outta that prison so I can get him back to the States, got it?"

"I understand that, but you have to understand, our public officials..."

"Screw your public officials," Caruso said, interrupting him. "They can be bought same's in the States. Ya jus' gotta find the right one."

'The man was not to be reasoned with', Fenwick thought as he listened to the mobster.

"Let us wait until I hear back from the lawyer. He may have some news which we can use to get your, er, colleague free."

"I don't care 'bout what yer mouthpiece sez. Jus' get him out. Now, what's the news on that last shipment?"

"Everything has gone well. As from last night, the shipment is currently enroute to the final destination that you specified. It should be there by tomorrow night."

"Good. I jus' got word from Chicago. They wanna another shipment. I'll get ya the order an' money in a day or two. Should be comin' across from the Island in a coupla days. I'll let ya know."

"So soon?"

"What can I say," he said. "People like ta drink. 'Sides, there's a big holiday comin' up. Big sellin' time an' Al wants to cash in."

"Alright. I'll begin to make delivery plans."

"Good. Don't forget...I want O'Leary out as fast as ya can spring 'im, got it?"

"Got it," Fenwick said as the line went dead.

He set the phone back on the table and stood looking at it for a moment before picking it up again and dialed a number.

"Is Lenny there?" he said when the call was answered.

"Not yet," the man at the other end said. "Too early."

"Tell him I want to see him this evening at six o'clock when he arrives."

"Yes sir."

He returned the receiver to the hook beside the mouthpiece and set the phone down again. As he turned and left the room, his mind was racing with the problems of finding a way to get O'Leary free and where he could find a boat to make the run to Miquolon.

* * *

At that exact moment, Lenny Purcell was walking down Queen Street on his way to meet a friend from his home who was up to the city for the day. He had received a call from home letting him know that Jack Aikens, an old friend, was coming to the city. Apparently, he was here for a hospital visit at the Halifax Infirmary. Lenny didn't get many chances to get away from his work for Fenwick so this would give him an opportunity to catch up on the news from home. He has been away almost two years now.

He didn't have many friends in the city, mostly by choice, since the only people he associated with were drunks, bootleggers, pimps, and whores. Mind you, he thought, there were a few of the swells that he took a bit of a shine to, but he knew outside of the world of speakeasies and illegal booze they wouldn't have the time of day for the likes of him. He didn't care since the money in his pocket came indirectly from them.

Just then Jerome Conway popped into his mind.

As he walked along, he thought about the past week since meeting up with Conway. He seemed likeable enough and was proving to be a good and reliable asset to the business. He was easy to work with and came across as being fairly smart. It seemed like they had some things in common, like their respective goals and aspirations for when Prohibition was over. The more he worked with him the more he found himself liking the man.

Shortly after he arrived at the Infirmary lobby area, Jack Aikens emerged from an elevator and walked up to him. They shook hands, happy to see each other again. Purcell realized that it had been more than eight months since he last saw his friend.

"So? What brung you to the hospital? Everythin' okay?" He asked as they walked back out onto the street.

"Yeah," Jack said. "Jus' in for a check up is all. The ole lady insisted."

"How is Meg?" Meagan was Jack's wife of fifteen years. The three of them grew up and attended school together.

"Same," was all Jack said. Purcell understood.

"When ya headin' back down?"

"I got a coupla hours. Whatcha thinkin'?"

"Did ys drive up or take the bus?"

"Bus."

"Good," Purcell said. "C'mon."

"Where ya takin' me? I gotta be back home before dark," Aikens said warily.

"You will be, stop worryin'."

Purcell led the way and fifteen minutes later they were sitting at a table in the speakeasy on Bishop Street with two glasses of beer in front of them.

"Ain't this 'spose ta be illegal?" Aikens asked, looking around the darkened room.

"Yeah," Purcell said, picking up his glass. "Good to see ya, buddy."

Aikens picked up his glass. "You, too."

Three glasses of beer later, the barman came over and looked at Purcell.

"Sorry ta interrupt but da boss is on the phone. Wants ta talk to ya," he said then walked away.

"Be back in a minute," Purcell said as he stood up and headed for the bar. He came back a few moments later.

"Gotta go," he said to his friend. "Let's finish up these beers then I'll get ya a cab to take ya to the bus station."

"Yeah okay. Ya know ya never did say what yer doin' here?"

"Best to not know. When ya get back home let the folks know everythin's okay an' I'll try an' get in touch soon."

"Alright. Anythin' else?"

"That's it. Ya ready?"

Once outside, they walked up to Barrington Street where Purcell was able to flag down a passing cab. He was so engaged with his friend that he failed to notice the black sedan that pulled away from the curb.

They both got in. He told the driver to head for the bus terminal. He dropped his friend off then ordered the driver to take him to Fenwick's house. He still didn't take notice of the black sedan.

When he arrived, Edward led him into the parlour as usual and went to get him a cup of coffee. Fenwick entered the room moments later.

"I have a problem," he said, crossing to a nearby chair and sitting down.

"Sir?" Purcell said.

"My schooner is currently unavailable, and I need to secure another vessel for a rush order. Are there any boats around that I can hire to make the run to Miquolon?"

"I'm not sure. How soon you need one?"

"Now, of course. Within twelve hours at the latest. Do you know anyone willing to make the run?"

"Maybe, I don't know for sure."

"It's got to be someone who can keep their mouths shut and willing to take the risk of crossing over from the island."

"Where will they have to make the delivery?"

"I will let you know as soon as you find me a boat. So? Do you have someone in mind? And do they have a boat that can handle a large load?"

"The only one that comes to mind right off is the one owned by the Joudreys."

"Are you serious?"

"Yes sir. Their boat is built for the open water and it's fast with enough cargo space for up to four hundred cases."

"That may be so, but aren't the Joudreys down in St. Margaret's Bay?"

"Yes sir. It would take an extra day for them to get to Miquolon, assuming good weather, but they could make it. An' we know them to be capable an' reliable."

"True," Fenwick said, thinking of the task ahead. "Alright. Call them and set it up."

"Sir. When do you want them to sail?"

"As soon as they have their boat ready for sea. Tell them to make sure they carry enough fuel for the crossing and that there will be fuel available in Miquolon for the return trip."

"What about money?"

"The job pays six hundred dollars plus their fuel."

"Right," Purcell stood up. "I better get on it."

"One more thing," Fenwick said.

"Sir?"

"I want you to go on with them on this run as well one other man. It is too big a run for just two men."

"Yes sir. I got a good man in mind who'd fit the bill. What's in it for him if he agrees to go?"

"Four hundred dollars."

"I think he'll go for that."

"Call me as soon as everything is ready. I will make the arrangements over in Miquolon at that time. Edward will drive you to where you need to go."

"Sir," Purcell said as he headed out. Edward was waiting by the door.

"Where to," he asked as we got in the car.

"Drop me down at the corner of Bishop and Barrington," Lenny said, settling into the plush seat.

When he reached the speakeasy and went inside, he noticed that Conway wasn't there. He went over to the bar and asked the barman if he had seen him today. The man shook his head, saying, "Da usual?"

"Yeah," Purcell said, looking around the room. He spotted a couple of men he recognized. A moment later the barman set a glass of beer in front of him.

Twenty minutes later, he realized he couldn't wait much longer for Conway to show up. The boss was waiting for him to call. He stepped away from the bar and headed for the office, telling the man inside to go out and get a coffee, he needed to room to himself.

Once he was alone, he reached for the telephone on the desk. It was one of those candlestick phones.

His first call was to Conway's place. Unfortunately, he was not in and the woman who answered said she did not know where he went or when he would be back. Damn it, he thought when he hung up.

His next call was to the Joudreys. They were out on their boat but were expected back shortly. He told the person on the other end to have Ken call him right away they came back. He gave them his number.

He sat there thinking through his options when the phone rang.

"Yeah?" he said, brusquely when he picked up the receiver. It was Ken Joudrey.

"Ya called?" Ken said into his ear.

"I need you and your brother for a job," he said.

"When?"

"Next twenty-four hours. That a problem?"

"Naw. We kin manage. Where we goin'?"

"Over to Miquolon."

"Miquolon! Jesus, we can't do that."

"Whaddya mean, you can't do it?"

"We ain't built ta make that sorta run, 'specially this time a year."

"Your boat is seaworthy. So what's the problem?"

'Yeah, she's built for open water but offshore not across da Strait, fer chrissake." He was referring to the Cabot Strait. The body of water between Cape Breton and Newfoundland with a notorious reputation for bad weather this time of the year. "It'd be risky 'nuff goin' over empty. It'd be more so comin' back. Sorry, Len, but we ain't willin' to risk our lives or boat."

"Shit," Purcell swore. "Know anybody got a boat willin' to take the job?"

"None comes ta mind."

"Okay. I understand."

"Hope this don't mean no more work."

"No, you're good. Talk to ya later." He hung up.

A moment after hanging up, the phone rang.

Hello?" he said when he answered.

"Ah, good. It's you," Fenwick said. "What progress have you made?"

"None. I can't find anyone willin' to make the crossin'."

"The Joudreys?"

"Nope."

"That's alright. I have just received word from the Americans. Seems our problem has resolved itself. They have a ship coming down the seaway from Montreal with a shipment on board. They have agreed to take delivery directly from the French supplier. Unfortunately, that will cut us out to a large degree. I will still broker the sale, mind, so..."

"That's great news, sir. Too bad we won't be able to make much on it."

"A lucky break, yes," Fenwick said, as he breathed a sigh of relief. "But not to worry. I have also made arrangements to include our stock in the Passage. I need the Joudreys to come up and make the run out to the ship. By the way, what is the total of the stash?"

"Close to five hundred cases and barrels all together," Purcell answered after a quick mental calculation. "So you're gettin' out of the liquor business?"

"Yes. I have concluded the time is ripe for a change of scenery, especially with the Americans taking a more, um, direct interest."

"Sure, I get that, but what about the rest of us?"

"The people we used, like the Joudreys, will go back to fishing, I suppose, or make new arrangements with whoever takes over the operation. As for you, I have a little bonus set a side."

"Bonus?"

"How would you like to take over the club down on Bishop Street?"

"Me? Run a speakeasy? Thanks, but no thanks. I ain't cut out to be a business owner. I'm a fisherman. I'll go back out on the water. I got enough put away so I might be able to get me another boat of my own."

"I see," Fenwick said. "How much would a boat cost?"

"I could probably get a good one for 'bout six grand," he said.

"And you have...?"

"'Bout forty-five or seven."

"Then let's make the bonus the balance of the cost then for your good service."

"Thanks. I don't know what to say."

"There is nothing to say. You earned it. Now, I need you to make a call to your cousin, Surrette. Tell him to contact me directly if he is interested in taking over the operation."

Purcell said he would, His cousin would probably jump at the chance.

He hung up the phone and sat back, his mind racing with the news he just received. His own boat. God damn, he said to himself. And his cousin was about to be given the chance to own the goose that lays the golden eggs.

Just then the door opened, and Lawrence Jenkins stepped inside.

Jenkins owned the building that housed the speakeasy. He was an older man in his early sixties with white hair and a bit of a belly on him. He was a widower: his wife of forty years had passed away a few years back during a flu epidemic that hit the province. To the best of Lenny's memory, he did not recall if Jenkins had any children.

Lenny was aware that shortly after Fenwick got into the liquor business, he was introduced to Jenkins and not long after that he made a deal with him to use his lower section of the house as a speakeasy for a percentage of the take. Jenkins, unlike many of Halifax's businessmen, jumped at the deal since he was himself into several shady operations of his own.

"You're looking quite satisfied with yourself," he said, rounding the desk and signalling for Lenny to vacate his chair.

"Got some bad news for ya Lawrence," Purcell said, moving to the front of the desk.

"Yeah? What's that?"

"The boss is packin' it in. Sellin' everythin' an' hightailin' it."

"No shit."

"No shit. He wants me to get Pete to contact him 'bout taken over."

"He selling everything?"

"I suppose so. I didn't ask."

"Don't be flip," he said with a sneer on his face. He and Lenny did not exactly get along. Theirs was strictly a business relationship which was fine with both of them.

"You think he'd be open to talking to me?"

"You got his number. I gotta go."

"What about you? You going to stay around?"

"Nope. When he's gone, so am I."

"Could make you a sweet offer."

"Not interested. I'm gettin' me my own boat an' then it's back on the water."

"Yeah? Well, give it some thought. Could be a good payday in it."

Purcell turned and left the office. Once he was outside, he walked back up to Barrington Street and caught one of the trams heading north. He was on his way to see his cousin, Pete Surrette. He settled onto an empty wooden bench seat, his mind spinning with a number of ideas, especially about buying his own boat.

Soon, he was sitting at a kitchen at Surrette's house on Acadia Street up in the north end of the city. There was a glass with about two ounces of rye whiskey in front of him.

"So? What's the big news?" Pete asked as he sat on one of the other wooden chairs.

"How much cash ya got put away?" Purcell asked.

He had called Pete Surrette and told him he was on the way up to see him with some big news. He was going to ask him if he was interested in taking over Fenwick's smuggling operation and the speakeasy. He considered how to make some money out of this deal for himself. If nothing else came out of his time working for Fenwick, he'd learned how to work the angles.

"Whaddya wanna know that for?" Pete asked.

"The boss got a deal he wants to offer ya."

"Go on."

"He's pullin' out of the business an' wants to sell off his operation. Interested?'

Pete whistled softly at what he just heard. His brain went into overdrive considering the possibilities and options.

"Whaddya mean? The whole operation? Contacts an' all, even the Yanks?"

"Yep. Everythin'," Lenny said, lifting his drink.

"Jesus. Yeah, I'm interested. Where does that put you?"

"I'm out too. Gonna buy a boat an' head back out on the water. Never was cut out for this smugglin' crap.

"Shit. Right. Whaddya figure your boss'll take?"

"Don't know. He said if you're interested to contact him direct."

"No kiddin'. So how do I get in touch with him?" Lenny pulled out a piece of paper with all the information Pete would need.

"First," he said, holding the paper on the table with his fingers. "There's the little matter of what's it worth to ya?"

"You shakin' me down?" Pete asked suspiciously.

"Let's jus' call it a service fee, sounds a lot better."

"And jus' how big is this, er, service fee?"

"Two thousand."

"What!"

"Ya heard me. Two grand. It's worth it an' you know it. Jesus, man, you'll get that back on your first deal an' then some. This deal is worth a shit load more than two grand an' you know it."

Pete sat a few moments considering what his cousin's offer, then said, "Deal."

"I want the money by the end of today, okay?"

"Done. I'll meet ya back here at five o'clock. It'll take me a little time to get the cash. That work for you?"

"At five," Lenny said, holding out his hand with the piece of paper in it. Pete took his hand and shook it, keeping the paper went he let go.

"Good luck," Lenny said. "Oh yeah, I got the impression he's in a bit of a rush to settle his affairs so you might have an edge when dealin' with him."

"Thanks," Pete said. He finished his drink then got up and headed out.

Lenny went back into the office to call Fenwick and let him know to expect a call from Surrette.

Chapter Ten

The man behind the wheel of the black sedan was Mike Fraser, an officer with the Royal Canadian Mounted Police stationed in Halifax. His immediate supervisor had singled him out for a special duty assignment the day before. He was to go undercover in mufti and take an unmarked car and park outside an address on Bishop Street. He was given a detailed description of a man he was to watch for and ordered to follow him, reporting any stops he happened to make.

Fraser made contact with the man that afternoon, only he wasn't alone. He was with another man. The two men flagged own a passing taxi and got in.

He drove carefully, making sure he stayed at least three cars back from the taxi with the men inside. It was driving north along Barrington Street, carefully dodging jaywalking pedestrians and the other traffic. Once they reached North Street it turn left. It turned out their destination was the bus terminal. The man with Purcell got out and they shook hands then the other man went inside the terminal.

The taxi then pulled away and headed back to the south end of the city. Finally, it arrived at a house on Young Avenue where it eased over to the curd and Purcell stepped out of the car. Fraser drove slowly down the boulevard to a break in the median where he pulled a u-turn, parking about five houses away. He took out his notebook and entered the address where Purcell went as well as a note on the man he saw him with. Twenty minutes later, Purcell came out and got into the homeowner's car with a driver who took him back to the speakeasy.

The RCMP officer had pulled over at the top of Bishop and watched as Purcell slipped into the alley leading to the club's entrance at the back of the building. He reached for the microphone under the dash.

"Car Two callin, over," he said into the microphone.

"Car Two, over," a man responded in a metallic scratchy voice.

"Car Two. Is Jacobs there? Over."

"Hold on, over."

A few minutes later the receiver sparked to life when Jacobs came online.

"Car Two. Jacobs here. What do have? Over," Jacobs said from the other end.

The driver depressed the send button and said, "Picked up Purcell at the Bishop address. He and another man caught a cab and went to the bus terminal where the other man got out. I then followed him to a residence on Young Avenue. He went inside and was there for about twenty minutes then left. I followed him back to Bishop Street. He's inside now, over."

"Excellent. Give me the address on Young Avenue, over," Jacob's asked.

The driver did as ordered, and Jacobs wrote down the information.

"Any further instructions, over?" the officer asked.

"No, call it a day for now and good work, thanks. By the way, what's your name? Over."

"Officer Mike Fraser, over."

"Yes, well, again, good work, over and out."

Douglas returned the microphone to its hook and sat back in his seat with a wide smile on his face. It was a good day, he thought.

Jacobs returned to his desk and pulled the phone over. He opened a drawer and took out a small book which contained special phone numbers. Flipping the pages, he finally found the one he was looking for and dialed it.

"Mrs. Chisholm," a woman said in his ear.

"This is Constable Phillip Jacobs with the R.C.M.P. My badge number is three-two-six."

"Yes, Constable, how may I help you."

"I need information for an investigation I am working on. Specifically, the name of the person living at one-forty-seven Young Avenue."

"Is that all you have to go on?"

"I'm afraid so. I am hoping that will enough."

"How do you know the occupants at that address have a telephone?"

"The neighbourhood would suggest they do."

"Ah, yes, I see," she said. "It will take a few minutes to look up that address. May I call you back?"

"That will be okay, you can call me at my direct number." He gave her the number to his phone. "I will wait on your call. Thank you for your help."

"Not at all," she said. "The telephone company is happy to assist the police at any time."

She called back thirty-five minutes later. The name of the occupant was Allister Fenwick.

The name was unfamiliar to him but none the less, he knew the man had to be someone withstanding and position in the city, if for no other reason than his address.

He checked the wall clock and saw that it getting on for ten o'clock in the evening. Too late to make any calls to the team members, so this news would have to wait until the morning.

The following morning, he called Walter McCarthy's office at eight o'clock. He knew McCarthy would be in since he always arrived at his office by seven.

"Fenwick? I seem to recall that name," McCarthy said after Jacobs had filled him in on his findings from the tail he put on Purcell. "A prominent businessman in the city, although I cannot say what line he is in."

"Odd, wouldn't you say?" Jacobs commented.

"Indeed. The more I think on it, that name has been mentioned in a number of connections among the people I know, notably in political circles. I will make some discreet enquires. It is most interesting that this man is apparently engaged in some dealings with a suspected smuggler, don't you think?"

"I was thinking the same thing. I think we should pass this along to Jerome, since he is working with Purcell now."

"Good point. I will see to it immediately when Miss Slaunwhite arrives. What further steps do you suggest we take at this point?"

"Well, I have a good man on Purcell at the moment. I suggest I put him on Fenwick instead since I don't believe there will be much more to be gained by staying on Purcell at this time. Besides, Jerome is closer to him than I am."

"I agree," McCarthy said.

"Have you made any progress on identifying who hired the lawyer sent to represent O'Leary?"

"Unfortunately, no. However, with this new Fenwick development...?"

"Good point. If he is somehow connected to the smuggling, he could very well be in a position to secure the services of that particular lawyer."

"All good points to be pursued."

"Right," Jacobs said. "I will call as soon as I have anything to report."

"As will I. Good luck."

"You, too." Jacobs returned the receiver to its hook.

* * *

Lenny was sitting at his usual table at the speakeasy going over Fenwick's news. The idea he would be out of the smuggling business didn't upset him in the least. He had been lucky so far and he made some money along the way. Now he was going to come into more money; enough to buy his own boat and return to his life back home with his family.

"Have you got a minute, Lenny," the barman called out.

He got up and went over to the bar.

"Yeah?"

"Call for ya." The man tilted his head toward the office door.

He went to the door and opened it. No one was inside. He saw the receiver sitting on the desk top next to the phone.

"Purcell," he said into the mouthpiece on the phone, holding the receiver to his ear.

"Lenny, it's me Charlie." Charlie Wilkes was one of the men who worked for Fenwick down in Jeddore. He knew him from his days fishing the Eastern shore.

"What's up?" he asked.

"'Member when you was down 'ere da other night an' I tole ya I taut I knew dat fella you was ridin' wit?"

"Yeah, so?"

"It finally come ta me. I was workin' a lobster string offa T'ree Fathom 'Arbour last season an' met up wit a coupla da lads was runnin' sum booze. Anyway, da cops shows up an' catches em all."

"So? What's that got to do...?" Lenny started to say.

"Yer mate was one a tha cops. 'E works fer da CPS," Charlie said, cutting him off.

"You sure 'bout that?"

"Yeah. 'E talked ta me fer a bit an' den let me go."

"Okay thanks," he said then hung up.

'Jesus Christ', he thought, considering what this meant. Here he thought Conway was a straight up guy, now it looked like he was probably going' to come down on him and put him in prison. Lenny sensed a growing feeling of anger in the pit of his stomach. ” We’ll see about that”.

He picked up the phone and called Fenwick.

“The Fenwick residence,” Edward said when the call was answered.

“It’s me, Lenny. I need to talk to the boss,” he said. “It’s important.”

“One moment.” He heard the phone being set down on the small table that was in the hall.

“Lenny,” Fenwick said when he came on the line. “Edward said that you have something important for me?”

“Yes sir,” Lenny said. “It’s Conway; the driver we took on. Looks like he’s an agent with the CPS.”

“WHAT! How do you know that?”

“One a the men down in Jeddore recognized him from a raid last year.”

“Good Lord. The man knows everything about our recent activities. How in the hell could this have happened?”

“There was no way to know he was with the CPS or any reason to suspect anythin’. He was in prison at the time he got in with us. Remember? It was the Joudreys who brought him in.”

“Obviously. He was planted there for just such an opportunity. This changes our plans drastically.” The line went quiet for several moments.

“Sir?” Lenny said.

"I am thinking," Fenwick said at last. "For the moment you stay by the phone; I assume you are at the bar?"

"Yes sir."

"Good. Wait there until I call back. By the way, have you contacted Surrette yet?"

"Yes."

"Call him back.. Tell him the offer on the table now is he can have the whole operation if he can raise the money to buy me out. I will try and get back to you in the next couple of hours."

"Yes sir." Then the line went dead. Lenny tapped the cradle a couple of times to re-establish a connection then dialed Pete Surrette's number.

* * *

As soon as Fenwick hung up, he headed for the room he used as his office. Antony Caruso was sitting in the leather chair in front of the large, polished oak desk reading several sheets of paper he held in his hand.

"We may have a serious problem," Fenwick said as he moved around the corner of the desk to his chair.

"What kinna problem?" Caruso asked, looking up from the page.

"It appears that new man we hired, Conway; the one with the truck. It seems he may be an agent working with the CPS."

"You sure 'bout that?" he asked, laying the pages on the desk.

"No, I am not sure. However, Purcell has the news from one of the people we use down in Jeddore. According to this person, he recognized Conway from a CPS raid last year."

"Wonder why he hasn't shut us down? He's gotta have enough information to cause a problem."

"I was wondering that myself. The only thing that I can surmise is the CPS must be amassing information for something bigger."

"Like what?"

"Us."

"Jesus, you might be right."

"It is a good thing then that our operation was set up to ensure we were insulated from discovery or, at the very least, far enough removed to allow us to shut down and leave if necessary."

"That may be so, but we're in the middle of a major shipment comin' down from Montreal, plus the load from Miquolon. Capone won't like losing that one too."

"I think we may have time. Our primary concern is what to do about Conway?"

"Simple. Kill him."

"Just like that?" Fenwick said, snapping his fingers. "We would have the police down on us like a tidal wave."

"Not if we do it right."

"I am listening."

"We get him to meet up with Purcell somewhere outside the city. Do him there an' then dump his body at sea."

"Hmmm. That plan has possibilities," Fenwick agreed, running the idea over in his mind. "I could arrange to move some product, say to Mahone Bay. And Purcell can get the Joudreys to stand by to take the body out on their boat. Although, I do not think I could get Purcell to do the actual killing. He does not seem to have the necessary temperament for such work. Maybe one of the Joudreys?"

"Don't worry 'bout that," Caruso said. "I'll deal with Conway. You, jus' set everythn' up."

"When?"

"The quicker da better."

Chapter Eleven

Lenny was still at the speakeasy enjoying a drink and a little female company. He got the first but before he could work on the second Fenwick called looking for him.

"Ah, Lenny," Fenwick said. "Just the man I want to talk to."

"Sir?" Lenny said. "What's up?"

"First, did you contact your cousin?"

"Yes sir. We jus' finished talkin' as a matter a fact."

"And?"

"He's definitely interested. I gave him the information to contact you."

"Excellent. Now to this Conway business. I need you to contact him and set up a run from the storage building on the Passage to Mahone Bay for tonight."

"You're kiddin'," Lenny said, catching himself for being so direct.

"You will go with him," Fenwick said, ignoring the remark. "Once you arrive in Mahone Bay, take the load to the dock where you will have the Joudreys standing by. One of the Americans will also be there; his name is Antony Caruso. He will take care of Conway. Then you will have the Joudreys take the body out to sea where they will dispose of it. Is all this understood?"

"Yes sir," he said.

"Jesus, Mary and Joseph', he thought. Murder. He knew something like this was a definite possibility, but he never expected to be part of it. A trickle of cold sweat ran down his spine.

"Once that is done, you will bring the load back to the Passage. Clear?"

"Yes. Clear, Whaddya want me to do with the with the truck?"

"I do not care. Keep it. Sell it. Give it to Jollimore. I leave it up to you. When you are done, come to the house in the morning at ten o'clock."

The line went dead, and Lenny hung up. He sat there staring at the phone in his hand for several moments, thinking about the task ahead. Could he really call a man up and make arrangements with him that would see the guy dead before the night was out? Could he live with himself knowing he would be responsible for the taking of a life?"

"I need a drink...a stiff one," he said to himself as he set the phone down.

Ten minutes later, he was back in the office dialing Conway's number, having resigned himself to carrying out the orders from Fenwick. Especially as he realized that if he didn't follow through, Caruso would likely kill him to.

"Hello," a now familiar woman's voice said.

"Is Jerry in?" he asked. "It's his buddy, Lenny."

"Yes, he is. Just a minute. I'll go get him."

He heard the phone as she set it down.

A minute or two later Conway came on the line.

"Hey," he said. "Whazzup?"

"Got a quick run for ya if yer free?" Lenny said, surprising himself at how calm he sounded.

"When an' where to?"

"Tonight. A hundred and fifty cases from the Passage down to Mahone Bay. The Joudreys'll meet us at that dock we were at before. I'll meet ya down at the ferry for the seven o'clock crossin'."

"Okay, see ya there." The line went dead.

Lenny tapped the receiver hook a couple of times for a new connection then called Fenwick's number. When he connected to him, he gave the boss all the information on the run to Mahone Bay. He said they would be down there between eleven and midnight. He heard Fenwick repeating the information to someone, probably Caruso.

"Good work. I will see you when you get back."

* * *

I hung up the phone and headed back to my room. Lenny Purcell offered me another quick run from the Passage to Mahone Bay, it was odd. A light load this time, only a hundred and fifty cases. As I walked down the hall, my gut was telling me that something seemed off this time. The memory of that fisherman down in Jeddore I saw talking to Purcell and looking at me came to mind. Maybe I was just feeling suspicious but that feeling had kept me alive so far, so I always took heed when it awakened.

The next morning I called the office as soon as I got up at six-forty-five. I knew I would get McCarthy right away since Nancy didn't usually get in before eight-thirty and this was a conversation I did not want her to hear.

"McCarthy," the boss said when he answered after the second ring.

"Mornin' sir," I said.

"Jerome. What news?"

"Purcell called late last night. Said he had another rush job; a hundred and fifty cases to go down to Mahone Bay tonight."

"I take it you have reservations about this run?"

"Yes sir, I do. Something 'bout it doesn't ring right."

"Such as?"

"The size of the load for one and the timing of the run. There's nothin' down that way that warrants a load of this size."

"Perhaps it is being moved to a vessel offshore?"

"Maybe," I said. "If so, this run is an unnecessary risk since he could just as easily have the Joudreys come up to the Passage an' pick up the load directly."

"I see your point," he said. "Then what do you think is going on?"

"There are a coupla possibilities, I think. One. There could be a customer down there that can take a load of that size, although to what end I don't know. I worked that part of the province long enough to know the liquor trade along the section of coastline wouldn't need that much booze."

"Go on. You said a couple of things."

"Sir. The other possibility is they discovered who I am working for an' intend to take me out."

"How in the world do you arrive at that possibility?"

"Remember my report on the last job down to Jeddore?"

"Yes, so?"

"Then you may remember my mentioning that I saw Purcell talkin' with one of the locals workin' for him and that they were eyeing me at the time."

"I don't see how...?" he started to say.

"On its own you're right but, taken with Purcell questioning me if I ever worked down that way before..."

"Ah, yes," he said, "I see why you are suspicious. Perhaps you should speak with Jacobs. I understand you asked him to find this man in Jeddore and to arrest him."

"Yes sir, I did."

"Well, as I understand, he has identified the man and has him in custody. So. What do you intend to do tonight?"

"Go ahead with it. Got no choice. If I don't go, they'll jus' try somethin' else. This way, I'll at least see it comin'." Or so I hoped.

"I agree. Perhaps it is time to move and bring this operation to an end. If nothing else, we will bring a number of key operators to trial and confiscate a substantial quantity of liquor. We may not net the ring leaders, but we can set their operations back significantly."

There was nothing I could add to his statement, so I just said, "Yes sir."

"Well, good luck tonight and please take great care of yourself. Miss Slaunwhite would be most upset if anything adverse were to happen to you and be more than a little upset with me."

"Sir. I will." He was one sly old fox. I hung up then went to the kitchen where Mrs. Pottie was at her usual post: the stove.

"Up early?" she said. "Tea's on the stove. I'll make you some eggs. Bacon or sausages?"

"Whatever's at hand, thanks." I went and poured a steaming mug of tea then sat at the table. We exchanged our usual banter while she prepared my breakfast.

When I finished eating, I got up, thanked her for another satisfying meal, then went out into the hall and picked up the phone again. This time it was to Phillip Jacobs.

"Jacobs," he said in my ear.

"Hi, it's me, Jerry," I said.

"Yeah, sort of recognized the voice. What's up?"

I quickly filled him in on my last call from Purcell and my overall concerns.

"I spoke with the boss earlier and he said you found that man down in Jeddore, is that right?"

"Yes. I contacted one of our men who patrols that section. Seems he knew straight away who I was talking about. Apparently, this man; his name is Charles Wilkes, by the way. Mean anything to you?"

"Not a damn clue who he is."

"Anyway, my man went to his house and took him in. He's actually cooling his heels in the city lockup. Matt's keeping an eye on him. Now that we got him, what do you want us to do with him? I can't keep him locked up indefinitely."

"Charge him under the Prohibition Act and as an accessory in a smugglin' operation. I'll provide the evidence at trial."

"Yeah, that'd work just fine. I'll begin processing him as soon we are done."

"Good," I said. "I don't suppose he said anythin'?"

"No. Just started screaming about being arrested without reason."

"Well, not to tell you your job, but if it was me, I'd lean on him, I mean lean hard. It's men like him that have a lot a names of others in the trade as well as boats being used."

"You're right...you don't have to tell me my job, but I get your point. I think with these charges, we may be able to get something useful. Back to your business for tonight. If you think something is going to happen to you do you want me to assign some men to back you up?"

"No. It may be nothin'. If it is I don't want to blow any chance to learn somethin'."

"Okay. It's your call. I'll stand by here until I hear from you one way or the other."

"Thanks."

* * *

I met up with Purcell at the ferry as planned.

Call it a sixth sense, or whatever, but for some reason, he seemed different somehow; like he had something on his mind. He climbed into the passenger side of the cab, and I drove onto the ferry.

"You, okay?" I asked as the boat eased away from its loading ramp.

"Huh? Yeah, sure Why ya askin'?" he said with a hint of edginess in his voice.

"Nothin' specific but ya don't seem to be yourself."

"It's nothin'. Had a rough night is all. Too much whisky an' beer."

"That'll do it for sure. So, what's up with this run?"

"Whaddya mean?"

"Kind a short notice an' a bit light. Didn't know there was any business down that way needs this much product?"

"Ain't for us to say. The boss sez we take a load somewhere, we take it; no questions."

"Okay, relax," I said, sensing he was getting a bit testy.

We made the rest of the crossing in quiet. Once we were on the Dartmouth side we headed for Eastern Passage. The whole operation took an hour and a half, and we made it back in time for the last ferry to Halifax. After disembarking from the ferry, I headed for the Bay Road which would take to the highway for the South Shore.

About a half mile from our destination outside Mahone Bay on an empty stretch of highway, Purcell told me to pullover. I assumed he wanted to drive the rest of the way. I downshifted and eased onto the soft shoulder and stopped.

"What's up?" I asked, looking at him. "I thought I'd take 'er down an' you'd drive back?"

Then I saw the gun in is hand. It was levelled at my gut.

"Jesus. What the hell's this?"

"I know you're a CPS agent," he said.

"A what! You're kiddin', right?"

"Wish I was. Charlie, our man down in Jeddore, fingered you. Is it true?"

It was at that moment I detected something in his voice. I decided to take a chance that this man was not a real villain or a killer.

"There's nothin' I can say so, the truth of it is, you're right; I am. So now what?

"Christ."

He was obviously struggling with an inner conflict.

"Listen to me, Lenny," I said, turning to face him. "You're in this up to your neck. There's no way 'round that, but as it stands right now as I see it, you'd be charged as an accessory. The worst you're facin' is a coupla years in jail. Pull that trigger an' it's the rope. Look, maybe there's a way we can help each other here."

"Jus' keep yer hands on the wheel," he said, holding the gun steady. "Whaddya mean, help each other?"

"Turn Crown's witness an' give up the ones runnin' everythin'. I'll back ya up an' push for the best break I can get ya."

"I don't know. He's waitin' for us right now."

"Who?"

"That Yank...Caruso. He's down there to kill you. The Joudreys are there too. They're 'spose to take your body out to sea an' dump it."

I had to think of something and fast. Looking out the windscreen, I could just make out the wharf and what I assumed was the Joudrey's boat.

"So," I said, looking back at him. "What's it goin' to be?"

"I'm screwed either way I go," he said, looking down the dirt track road.

"Maybe, but don't forget, one of your choices could get ya the rope."

"Shit. Alright. Ya got a deal." He lowered his gun. "But we can't turn back now. They spotted the truck." He nodded out the window.

I followed his gaze and saw one of the Joudrey brothers walking towards us and waving us down. I pulled out my gun and flicked the safety off then put it in the waist of my pants.

"Right. You ready?" I asked, taking my foot off the brake.

"Let's get it over with."

I drove slowly down to the dock area. Ken Joudrey stood at the head of the dock. I saw his brother, Bill, standing at the stern of their boat. There was no sign of the American.

"Take 'er over there," Ken said, pointing to the side of his boat.

I rolled onto the wooden wharf then stopped beside the boat. Lenny got out and went to the back of the truck. I shut the motor down then got out. As I stepped to the rear, I heard Ken and Lenny talking.

"What's with da gun?" Ken said. Lenny still had his pistol in his hand when got out of the truck.

"The gig's up," he answered, raising the gun.

"Whadda fuck ya sayin'?"

"It's over. Everythin'. All of it an' all of us." He tilted his head in my direction when he heard me approaching. "He's CPS, an' knows everythin'."

"Jesus, Lenny," I said, reaching for my gun. Then suddenly, there was a searing pain at the back of my head then total blackness.

I didn't know which was worse – the boat pounding through the swells or the blacksmiths inside my head using my brain as an anvil. Whatever it was succeeded in bringing me back to consciousness. As the fog cleared and my vision began to work normally again, I saw that I was lying on the deck of the Joudreys' boat with my hands bound behind me. I looked around, shaking my head trying to remember.

I was lying on the deck between the gunwale and a small square hatch cover. Each time the boat plowed into another rolling swell it sent a deluge of seawater crashing over me. The jolt from the cold water ran through me which helped to clear my head. I lay there, soaked to the skin, and surveyed the situation.

Taking in my surroundings, I saw another body lying below my feet. I quickly identified it as Lenny Purcell, or what was left of him. A thinning stain of blood was being washed over the deck by the incoming seawater. The right side of his head looked like it had been smashed away. I realized then he had been shot in the head. I tilted my head a bit and saw the Joudreys and Anthony Caruso standing under the dodger covering the small wheelhouse. Ken was steering the boat while his brother and Caruso held onto something as they all tried to keep their feet under them.

"'Ere," I heard Ken yell. "Git down below and see if ya kin get more revs outta da engine."

Bill let go of the post he was holding and moved unsteadily towards where I was lying. When he saw I was back in the land of the living he called out, "He's awake."

They barely heard him over the roar of the wind and the crashing of the bow against the waves. Caruso turned, giving me a quick glance. He didn't look to be in any hurry to let go of his piece of the cabin as he turned back to look out the water-streaked window.

Bill reached the hatch cover and bent down. I lashed out with one of my free legs, landing a solid kick to his rib cage.

"Aaaaaa," he cried out, buckling over. "Ya bastard."

He managed to stand up and drew his knife from the sheath on his belt.

"I'm gonna gut ya fer dat." He was having a hard time maintaining his balance with the boat tossing around and holding his ribs.

I braced myself for the attack, trying to work out some way to protect myself with my hands tied. Then suddenly he jerked back as I saw three neat holes rip through his shirt. He dropped the knife as he fell to his knees, blood welling up and out of his mouth. Then he keeled over, falling onto his face...dead.

A moment later, I watched as the inside of the wheelhouse seemed to splinter and disintegrate as a burst of bullets ripped into the wood. Then I heard the sound of someone's voice blaring through a megaphone.

* * *

I awoke two days later in a private room in the Infirmary Hospital. The first thing I noticed was my bandaged head and the dull throbbing ache. Then I saw Nancy sitting in a visitor's chair and suddenly the pain didn't seem important anymore.

"What happened?" I croaked; my throat felt bone dry.

She stood up, came over to the bed, and poured a glass of water for me. As she put the rim to my lips, she said, "Sssh. Take a drink. You've been unconscious for two days."

"I don't understand," I said after taking a couple of swallows of water. "How'd...?"

"There's lots of time to fill in the blanks, my love. For now, rest." She smiled tenderly as she put the glass on the side table.

"Not yet," I said, my voice sounding tired. "I need to know. All I remember is gunfire then...nothing."

"Maybe I can fill in some of the details, if you're up to it?" It was Phillip Jacobs. He had just stepped into the room.

"Yeah, go on," I said, looking at him as he stood beside Nancy. She was holding my hand.

"Well, I can't account for your head injury," he started, "I'm guessing you took that hit back on the dock."

"Yeah, I recall getting hit on the back of my head now that you mention it."

"Near as I have been able to get out of the Joudreys so far is your cover was blown and the leader behind this operation set a trap for you. The plan was the American was supposed to kill you they were there to dump your body out at sea."

"Oh my God!", Nancy gasped, squeezing my hand.

"What about Purcell? How'd...?" I started to ask.

"According to Ken Joudrey, after you were attacked, it was his brother who hit you, by the way. Anyway, after that Purcell tried to shoot his gun, that's when the American, Caruso, joined in and shot him in the head. He was dead before he hit the ground."

"Poor bugger. I had convinced him to rollover on the lot of them. So how come you turned up when you did?"

"Pure luck," Phillip said with a slight smile. "A call came in from an informant, alerting us that the Joudreys had sailed and were headed for Mahone Bay. Something inside me said I better tag along, knowing what you were up to. We intercepted them about four miles outside the Bay and they were making a run for it. That's when your people opened fire. Unfortunately, the American decided to try and shoot it out without success."

"So all we got for all that bloodshed are the Joudreys," I said sourly.

"Not exactly."

"Huh?"

"We arrested the leader of the smuggling operation a day ago."

"How did you pull that off?"

"Good old fashion police work and a little of that luck I mentioned a moment ago. But that's enough for now. You need to get rest so you can come back. I'm sure McCarthy will have everything you need to know. Just get back on your feet, okay?"

"Okay," I said. "By the way, who was it?"

"His name is Allister Fenwick."

I watched as Jacobs left the room leaving me and Nancy alone. She let go of my hand and pulled a chair closer and sat down, taking my hand again.

"Listen," she said, "and don't interrupt me. If I am going to spend the rest of my life with you, you will have to put in for a desk job. I will not grow old with the fear you may be killed. Agreed?"

I looked deep into her beautiful eyes and smiled "Agreed."

Epilogue

I spent three more days in hospital with a major concussion. When I was released from the hospital, I returned to my room at Mrs. Pottie's. As soon as she saw my injury she went straight into 'mother' mode and set about caring for me. I stayed on with her for another few days, during which time I had the opportunity to meet her husband who came home. I moved out two days later with the promise to keep in touch.

Over the intervening days, I learned more of the events that transpired from that fateful night in Mahone Bay.

McCarthy, in cooperation with Jacobs and Murphy, executed a massive series of raids throughout the province netting almost a half million dollars in contraband liquor and shutting down numerous operations. The speakeasy on Bishop Street was closed and the crews in Jeddore and Eastern Passage were arrested, and eight boats confiscated.

As for Allister Fenwick. He was arrested and charged under the Prohibition Act, smuggling and conspiracy to import contraband alcohol for the purpose of selling it in the domestic market. The Crown also seized all his assets and holdings. It turned out that his network of political connections very quickly deserted him which led him to make a deal with the Crown in exchange for more lenient sentencing. The Crown, upon learning of his British origins, decided to sentence him to ten years in prison or accept deportation. He accepted the offer.

The information elicited from Fenwick on his American dealings were sent on to John Lee which he used to effect in Chicago, New York, and Boston.

Sean O'Leary went to trial for murder and was convicted. He is presently serving time in Kingston Prison awaiting his date with the hangman.

As for me; when I returned to work I submitted my request for a transfer to other duties other that those in the field. McCarthy was sorry to see me quit that part of the service but conceded that I did more than my share, besides, my usefulness as an undercover agent locally was finished.

Nancy and I married four months later and have settled into a happy life in Ottawa where I am posted as a training officer.

The events of that night still haunted my dreams when I realize just how close I came to dying. But that's over now and the doctors say I'll be up and out of here in another day. As for the dreams, I'm pretty sure they'll go away...with help from Nancy, who has made it clear that she intended to replace them with more pleasing ones.

The End

Author's Note

The Volstad Act was passed by the United States in 1918 and enacted in January 1920 which signaled the beginning of the Prohibition Era and what was to be known as 'The Roaring Twenties'. The Canadian Government passed similar legislation, with the Temperance Act, in 1878 (the Scott Act) which granted authority and enactment options directly to the Provinces and Yukon.

In the 1920s, fishermen from the Maritime Provinces could no longer make a living from fishing due to over stocks and reduced prices. Many opted to use their boats to collect loads of illegal liquor from 'mother' ships positioned offshore outside the three-mile limit and transporting them to designated landing spots ashore where they were received for transshipment to inland markets.

However, that changed in 1925 when an agreement between the United States and many of the other maritime nations redefined the territorial offshore limit from three miles to twelve miles. During this time there were three main ports in Nova Scotia heavily engaged in this trade: Halifax, Lunenburg, and Yarmouth.

Most of the liquor originated from St. Pierre and Miquelon, French owned islands off the south-west coast of Newfoundland. This was also the delivery destination for liquor from the Caribbean, Europe, and Canadian producers who were prohibited from selling their product into any market in Canada or the United States. where the purchase or sale of alcohol as illegal.

Terms used in this story

CPS - The Canadian Customs Preventive Service Fleet in the Maritime Provinces and Eastern Quebec. This agency was responsible for the interdiction, interception, and seizure of contraband on or over water.

Rum Runner - A person engaged in transporting illegal liquor from a ship positioned outside the three-mile limit (later the twelve-mile limit) to receiving vehicles on shore for distribution to land based users/sellers.

Rum Row - Area designated by US Coast Guard where ships, schooners, and small tramp steamers waited after arriving with cargoes of liquor from the Caribbean or the Bahamas or the French owned islands of St Pierre & Miquelon off the southwestern coast of Newfoundland.

Speakeasy/Blind Pig/Boozecan Colloquial terms for illegal drinking establishment. Speakeasies were the most notable as these were more like nightclubs frequented by society figures and criminals alike. The most famous was the Cotton Club in Harlem, New York.

Sources

Public Archives of Nova Scotia: The Rum Running Years, Ted R. Henniger 1981

Preview of Detective John Robichaud Series

Robie's War
Chapter One

Winter 1942

It was a cold, clear night. A brilliant white moon cast an unearthly light over the snow-covered landscape; a paved road cut through the whiteness in a black line. Two cars, their engines idling, sat in the shadows of a side road three miles southwest of Hilden, outside the town of Truro. Four men sat in one car armed with sawed off shotguns and handguns. They all wore scarves over their faces. In the lead car, two men sat watching a man standing twenty feet away near the road. Suddenly he waved his arm then dashed back to the car and got in.

"Here they come," the man behind the wheel said, pulling his scarf over his nose.

A few minutes later, two three-ton trucks rumbled past.

"Right," said a man in back. "Let's go."

The driver shifted into first gear and let out the clutch, pushing the accelerator pedal down. The rear tires dug in, sending a spray of loose gravel and dirt as it moved off. The other car immediately followed behind. The cars overtook the lorries within minutes.

The lead car raced ahead of the lead lorry and turned across the road, blocking the oncoming vehicle, causing it to slam on its brakes; the other lorry stopping behind it. The car with the four armed men inside stopped behind the last lorry. They got out and rushed to either side of the vehicles, aiming their weapons at the men inside. The two vehicles were surrounded by the armed men. One of the hijackers stepped to the lead truck and aiming his pistol at the driver, barked, "Out. Now. No funny business, hear, or I'll shoot ya dead. An' bring da manifests with ya."

The men sitting in the cabs of the lorries slowly got out with their hands up. One of the hijackers grabbed the papers from two of the men and passed them to another man. Two of the thieves led the four truckers to the side of the road while two of their confederates climbed into the cabs and started to drive away. Then they backed away to the waiting cars and got in, keeping their weapons on the truckers.

"Have a nice walk back, fellas," one of the hijackers said, laughing. The whole operation took less than five minutes.

"That was a piece a cake, eh, boss?" the driver said from the front seat.

"Yeah," the man in back answered. "Gotta like these people. Crazy ideas 'bout no guns."

"No kiddin'. Back home we'd've had to take 'em. out"

"How long before we get back to da barn?"

"Maybe a half hour or so, dependin' on da road," the driver said. It snowed again earlier today."

"Right. Turn on the overhead so I can take a look at what we got."

"Okay."

Three hours later the four truckers were sitting in the local detachment of the Royal Canadian Mounted Police in Truro. They had been picked up about an hour after the hijacking by a passing farmer on his way to Bible Hill.

"Okay," said the uniformed Mountie. "Let's go over what happened one more time."

"Jesus, man," one of the men said, setting the mug of hot tea on the desk. "How many more times we gotta tell ya?"

"Just tell me again how it went down. The sooner you do, the sooner I can get you men back home."

"Like we tole ya already; we left da rail yard last night 'round ten o'clock. We jus' finished loadin' five hunnerd boxes, two-fifty per truck, headed fer Halifax. We was hopin' to make Halifax for a top up of diesel an' a break. Then suddenly, these two cars charged us an' blocked da road jus' a coupla miles da other side of Hilden. Next we know, we's walkin' down a dark, cold road, leastwise 'til dat farmer come by."

The officer took down notes as the trucker recounted the events of the theft for the third time.

"Do you know what was in the boxes?"

"Not sure, but dere was red crosses painted on dem."

"And you all agree to what he just said as to what happened?" he asked, looking at the other men.

"Yup," one of the other men said. "dat's 'bout the size of it."

"Right." The officer closed his notebook and stood up.

"Now what?" the initial speaker asked. "Whadda we do now?"

"You'll stay here until daybreak then I'll arrange transport for you back to the city. It'll probably be a military transport. They'll deliver you to the Naval Intelligence office. They're going to want to talk to you before you can go home. We'll see you have a good breakfast first. Now, come with me."

He led them to the back of the building where there were two empty cells.

"Sorry it couldn't be any better," he said, apologetically. "But it's warm and dry. The door'll be open, and the toilet is just down there. Get some sleep."

The constable went back to his desk and picked up the phone, dialing the number of RCMP headquarters in Halifax. When he got through, he was connected to the duty officer and made his report. By the time he finished, transport was being arranged for the four men and Naval Intelligence was alerted. He hung up, went to the door of the station, locked it, and then headed to the back and his room.

* * *

It was a cold morning, and I was heading for the police station located under City Hall. I was sitting on the hard wooden seat of the tramcar, looking out the window which was wet from condensation formed by the body heat of so many people in overcoats. The moisture obscured my view of the passing parade of people on the street. I didn't mind that much; I knew I would see enough of them as the day wore on. In some way it was a relief not to see clearly, a sort of brief reprieve.

My name is John Robichaud, Robie to my friends. I'm a detective on the Halifax Police force. This was my second go round with war, having served in, and surviving, the last one. I remembered them saying this was the one to end all wars with a twinge of sadness as I looked up at the crush of young men in uniform crammed in the tram. They seemed younger than in my day and just as full of national fervour.

When I mustered out of the army I wandered around for a while before landing in Boston where I met a former comrade who convinced me to join the Boston Police Department.

I served on the force for several years as a beat cop in South Boston; one of the tougher neighbourhoods in the city. I soon discovered I liked police work. Then the time came when I decided it was time for me to go back home to Cape Breton in Nova Scotia. However, I soon realized I couldn't live in the small community of my birth anymore and ended up in Halifax, the capital of the province.

I applied to, and was accepted into, the police force. I paid my dues as a patrolman walking a beat in the tough waterfront area. During that time, I got lucky and worked on a couple of cases with the detective squad, demonstrating a talent for detective work. This led to a promotion as head of the detective department. I guess Daniel Morrison, my boss, thought my background in Boston made me the best choice.

It was coming up to the second full year of the war and Halifax was running full out as the main port of assembly for men and materials destined for England via convoys, especially now that America had entered the war. This proved to be fertile ground for the local criminal element: bootlegging, illegal moonshiners, prostitution, thefts, and black marketeering, all these on top of the usual business of city policing: drunkenness, public rowdiness, vagrancy. Although, theft, especially from the docks, had become our main issue.

The crowded tramcar rattled down Barrington Street heading for the shipyards in the north end. It was only seven-thirty, and the street was already full of people making their way to work or idling in front of the closed shops. I absentmindedly pulled my arm across the wet pane of glass and looked out onto the passing scene: people, both civilian and military, moving like a choreographed dance past each other, and vehicles – mostly trucks – inching along as they tried to get to their destinations.

The tram finally arrived at my destination, the corner of Duke and Barrington Streets. I exited the tram and stepped over a small snowbank onto the sidewalk. Once the tram moved off, I crossed over to the other side of the street, weaving through the traffic.

I saw the usual crowd of uniformed police officers milling about before starting their shifts and waved to a few I recognized. Inside, a crowd of people; the usual mob of merchants, or landlords with complaints, and servicemen waiting to be charged for some minor infraction or other. These days, the busiest cop was the desk officer.

I pushed through the press of people and made my way to the far side leading to the squad room. Before I escaped down the hall, a young beat cop stopped me.

"Sorry to bother ya, sir, but a woman's come in lookin' for ya," he said. "The desk sergeant said to put 'er in the squad room."

"For me, you say?" I asked.

"Yeah. He sez she asked for you specifically."

"She didn't say what it was about?"

"Wouldn't know," he said, shaking his head.

"Okay. Thanks."

I headed down to the door of the squad room and went inside. Pete, my partner, wasn't in yet but I spotted two men sitting at their desks. The night shift, busy writing up their reports. A woman sat in a chair beside my desk. I had no idea who she was or how she claimed to know me.

"I'm Detective Robichaud," I said. "I was told you asked for me?"

"That's right," she said. "I need help. My daughter is missing." I heard the hint of a French accent.

"Okay, but how did you come to ask for me?"

"Elsie Paul. I'm her daughter, Marie." She said this as if it explained everything. In a way it did. Elsie Paul was my grandmother on my mother's side. My mother was Mi'kmaq and had married outside the tribe. I hadn't been in contact with that side of my family since I left to enlist in the last war, and I hadn't been back to my hometown since nineteen-twenty-three. This woman was my aunt by blood.

"I see," I said, looking at her.

She wore a heavy wool overcoat that hung down below her knees above a pair of winter boots. Her hands were covered with knitted wool gloves and held a purse on her lap. I could see she was in her late forties with graying hair peeking out from under the bandanna. As I looked at her face, I could see some of her Indian features: slightly high cheekbones, dark eyes, thin lips. She reminded me of my mother.

"Can I get you a cup of coffee? Tea?"

She shook her head.

"Why do think your daughter's missin'?" I asked, pulling out my chair and sitting down.

"I haven't heard from her in a week now."

"Do you live here in the city?"

"No. I come up from Wagmitkuk two days ago."

I knew Wagmitkuk was a Mi'Kmaq settlement near Margaree in Cape Breton about twenty miles from my family's home.

"I take it your daughter came to the city."

She nodded. She spoke as many natives did. Economically. Saying only what mattered without excitement or emotion in their voice. Most whites I've known see this as a sign of their lack of intelligence, but I knew differently.

"When?"

"Six months ago. She came for work."

"What's her name and age?" Most Indians have taken Christian names in order to fit in and find work.

"Catherine. She's twenty."

"Do you have a local address for her?"

"She had a room on Creighton Street," she said, pulling out an envelope and passing it to me. "This was her last letter."

I noted the return address written in the upper left corner and the postmark dated three weeks ago. I removed the letter from inside. It was just a single page, and I quickly scanned it. There was nothing unusual in it, just what you'd expect to see in a letter from a daughter to her mother.

"Did she get a job?"

"Worked at the hotel in the kitchen as a pot scrubber," she said, nodding.

"Which hotel?"

"The Lord Nelson."

"You said you last heard from her a week ago so, what makes you think somethin's wrong?" I asked.

"She always calls on Saturday. This time she didn't."

Saturday; four days ago.

"Maybe she was workin' or steppin' out with a fella."

She shook her head.

"I talked to the hotel. No one has seen her since last Friday. She is a good girl and didn't have a boyfriend."

I sat looking at her, considering what she was telling me. Normally I would chalk it up to a girl loose and on her own in a city full of eligible young men except, according to her, the hotel said she hadn't been at work since she left last week.

I knew the native community was very small here in the city and, like the blacks, generally took work wherever they could, usually in low menial jobs: maids, cleaners, porters, and the like. Like the black population, natives tended to stay pretty much to themselves. I knew that there were those in the white community who took a shine to the novelty of getting it on with Indian women.

"I don't suppose you have a picture of your daughter?"

She dug into her purse again and pulled out a black and white photograph and gave it to me. I eyed the image.

"That was taken a year ago on her birthday," Mrs. Paul said.

I eyed the image: a pretty young woman standing outside a house in a sweater and skirt. She looked happy.

"Can I hang on to this?" I asked.

She nodded.

"Leave this with me for now. We'll look into it an' let you know if we turn up anythin'. Where can I reach you? You stayin' here in the city?"

"At the YWCA," she said, giving me a phone number. "Will it take long?"

"Hard to say, but we'll get on it."

She stood up and said, "I will be here until I find out."

I stood up and escorted her to the stairs leading up to the parking lot in the Grand Parade ground. It would easier for her to get to the street and avoid the confusion out front. I watched her go, thinking about how stoic she was, typical of Indians; don't show any emotion.

When I returned to my desk, I saw that Pete had arrived. Pete Duncan has been my partner since the outbreak of the war. He's a good cop and detective, and we have become close friends. A good man in a tough situation as I came to learn from working on several high risk cases.

"Mornin'," he said. "Did I jus' see you walkin' a woman out?" He came over and sat on the corner of my desk.

"Yeah," I said, sitting down. "She reported her daughter missin'."

"That so?"

I passed him the photograph which he took and looked at.

"Pretty girl."

"The woman was her mother. Sez she hasn't heard from her for a week. The girl came here from Cape Breton six months back lookin' for work. Sez she got a job at the Lord Nelson in the kitchen doin' scullery work. Accordin' to her, the hotel told her the girl hasn't been at work for over week."

"Maybe she quit," Pete said.

"Mother didn't say so," I said "Take a run up there an' check it out. I gotta go up an' see the boss on another matter. Take the picture with you. Talk to the kitchen staff, see if any of them know anythin'. You know the routine."

"Okay."

I turned and headed for the stairs leading up to the second floor where Lieutenant Morrison, the Police Chief and my boss, had his office. He was in his late fifties and showed it. These days he works primarily as an administrator but don't let that fool you; he's all cop. He came up through the ranks from beat cop back in the twenties during the rum running days and prohibition to detective. I liked working for him.

When I reached his office, I rapped on the glass panel and opened the door. He was sitting behind his desk as usual; a large oaken beast. He was leaning on his forearms as he looked up when I stepped inside, closing the door behind me.

Sitting in one of the two chairs in front of it was my friend, Lieutenant Commander Michael Parks. Parks was with the Royal Canadian Navy and head of naval intelligence with Atlantic Command. He was a young good-looking man. Average height and fit. He was educated in England before the war and returned to Toronto in nineteen-thirty-five. He enlisted in the navy as a Second Lieutenant and was quickly reassigned to intelligence. We had worked on several over-lapping cases in the past.

"Take a seat," Morrison said in his usual direct manner.

"Hello Robie," Parks said as I sat down. "Good to see you again."

"Yeah, you too," I said, glancing from one to the other. Michael being here meant I was about to be given another assignment involving his department.

"Michael is here with the approval of the Mayor. He has a problem and thinks he could use our help," Morrison said, looking at Parks.

"Right." He turned slightly in his seat to look directly at me. "As you are no doubt aware, the port has been receiving higher volumes of war materials and goods for overseas since America came into the war. This has led to a marked increase in pilfering and outright large-scale thefts both here in the port as well as outside in the rural areas, especially on the highways. There has been a number of transport truck hijackings recently. Normally, this would be a matter handled by the RCMP but in the last two incidents the cargoes stolen were pharmaceuticals and military ordinance which, of course, landed them on my desk."

"Let me guess, you don't have the manpower to investigate."

"Correct," he said. "Nor do we have the jurisdiction or authority to undertake such an investigation outside the limits of the port. Normally, Phil would work with the local authorities but in this instance, we have been ordered to get involved since the items stolen were for military use."

Phil Mulroney was with the Royal Canadian Mounted Police force. He had been assigned to Halifax at the start of the war to assist with port security. A Sergeant at the time, he has since been promoted to Inspector. He and I have worked a couple of cases since he came here, and I have come to learn he was a very capable policeman. We have become very good friends.

"Okay, I get that, but we don't have any jurisdiction or authority outside the city either."

"That's being dealt with by the Mayor and the local RCMP Commissioner," Morrison said. "We'll be working jointly with Parks' office and the local RCMP detachment."

"And that would be where?" I asked.

"Truro," he answered. "The last hijacking took place between there and here a day ago. According to the four men in the trucks, they were intercepted by two cars with heavily armed men inside near Hilden. It's located somewhere between Truro and Brookfield. The hijacking happened at approximately three in the morning."

"Anybody hurt?"

"Fortunately, no," Parks added.

"I guess it had to happen sometime," I said. Parks gave me a funny look. "Organized gangs comin' here lookin' for easy money. Look at the operation they ran. Two cars. Plenty of well-armed men. I'm guessin' the whole operation took less than five minutes. There's nothin' operatin' like this that I know 'bout here or anywhere else in the province."

"That was what the drivers reported. One car sped ahead and forced them to stop while the other stayed at the rear. They then forced the men out of the trucks and replaced the drivers with two of their own and sped off. How did you work it out that it had to be an organized gang?"

"I remember a similar operation back when I was with the Boston police. Happened back during Prohibition. It was common practice for rival gangs to hijack each other's liquor runs."

"You think there might be an American crime organization behind this?"

"Hard to say, but I doubt it. I haven't heard anythin' indicatin' the American mob is here in the province but that doesn't mean it isn't the case. If I had to make a guess, I'd hafta say it's more likely an operation this big would be run by one of the mobs outta Montreal, maybe even Toronto. After all, there's a lot of high-end material travelin' to the port."

"So, why not the States?" Morrison asked.

"Wouldn't make any sense," I said, looking at him and shaking my head. "If the Americans were involved, they'd likely hit the loads closer to home, not all the way up here."

"I see. Right. I'm attaching you to Parks' department to help them with this situation. You working anything I don't know about at the moment?"

"A woman came in before I came up to report her daughter missing. I sent Pete up to where she works to ask around."

"Good. He can run with it while you do this."

"Yes sir, but I'd like to keep in touch with him. I got a personal connection to it."

Morrison raised an eyebrow questioningly.

"The girl's mother is related to my family."

"Alright," he said. "But putting a stop to these hijackings takes priority."

"Yes sir."

Both Michael and I stood up and headed out of the office.

"When do you want me to come down?" I asked.

"If it is okay with you, let's meet up for lunch, and I'll give you a rundown on what we have so far. Meanwhile, I'll set up a workplace for you."

"Sounds good. Will I be workin' directly with you or Phil?"

"Phil. I'll oversee the operation, as usual. Best if I stay out of your way. You and Phil are so good at what you do, especially together."

"Right. I'll meet you at noon. I got a coupla things I gotta clean up before I take off. By the way, where do want to meet up?"

"In the canteen," he said. "I'll have Phil join us."

The canteen was located in the Naval Headquarters Building down at the lower end of Barrington Street. The food was pretty good all things considered.

"See you then."

We shook hands then he headed out.

"Hang on a moment," Morrison said as I headed for the door.

"Sir?" I said, sitting back down.

"This business is serious," he said. "I got word that there have been similar thefts down in Sydney. The last hit two of the men transporting the goods were shot. One was killed, the other is in hospital in critical condition. If this is mob run out of Montreal, then it could be dangerous and must be shut down. I don't want these people setting up shop in this city."

"Yes sir," I said.

"I'm authorizing you to use whatever force necessary to ensure they get the message that they aren't welcome here. Understand?"

"Yeah, I understand." I knew what he was telling me. He knew I wasn't squeamish about using my weapon when necessary and I was to treat this situation as necessary from the outset.

Chapter Two

Pete Duncan drove down Sackville Street to South Park Street and turned left. The street was pretty clear of snow since the snowplows had been out overnight; two-foot-high snowbanks lined the side of the street on either side. Traffic was moderately heavy at this time of day, most of it being military. Not all that surprising since this part of the street went between the army fort at Citadel Hill and Royal Artillery Park.

Pete was coming up on thirty-seven but still looked good. Tall and well built, he held his own when dealing with the weekend rowdies and hard boys. He was married to a woman he met while working his first serious case with Robie back in thirty-nine. Now he was soon to become a father.

He had been Robie's partner since to outbreak of the war. They had worked on a number of hard cases involving the IRA and German spies which lead to them sharing several dangerous moments together. Still, it was a good partnership based on trust and friendship. So, when Robie told him to head up to the Lord Nelson Hotel and talk with the kitchen staff about a missing girl he didn't hesitate. Besides, he thought, he was ready for something more interesting than dealing with the constant 'bitchin' of the general public about sailors, merchantmen and now, Yanks.

He pulled into the drop off area of the Lord Nelson Hotel. He got out and headed for the entrance. A uniformed doorman in an ankle length overcoat stepped toward him with a raised arm.

"You can't park your car there," he said, pointing at his car.

"Police business," Pete said, showing his badge.

"Sorry," the man said, stepping back to the door and opening it for him.

"Thanks." Pete entered the lobby, which was crowded with businessmen, military officers, and a few well-dressed women.

He made his way through the press of people crowding the front desk; people trying to check out or in, keeping the three men behind the desk busy. He managed to get to a spot at one end and, waving his badge at the first clerk to look his way, called him over.

"The Manager's office?" he asked when a young man leaned in his direction while holding his hand out to an army captain.

"Up on the mezzanine level," he answered, pointing above his head.

"Thanks."

He pushed his way out of the crowd and headed for the stairs to the right of the desk. He walked over the thickly carpeted floor and stairs to the mezzanine level, admiring the opulence of the lobby: thick upholstered Morris chairs placed around the lobby with three-legged redwood tables beside them. Most had brass lamps with crystal shades. Grand paintings adorned the walls and a crystal chandelier hung from the ceiling. It radiated old world prestige and elegance.

He stopped a bellboy and asked directions to the Manager's office. The boy pointed the way. When he found the door, he opened it and stepped inside.

Compared with the outer area the office seemed somewhat spartan. There were several filing cabinets along a wall, three chairs along another and a desk in front of a closed door with an attractive woman sitting behind it. She wore a skirt and a pale blue blouse with full sleeves and a thin black tie down the front.

"Yes. May I help you?" she said in a formal tone, looking up from some paperwork on the desk.

"Detective Sergeant Duncan, Halifax Police Department," he said, showing her his badge. "Is the Manager in? I'd like a few words."

"May I ask what this is about?"

"I'm lookin' into a matter involvin' a missin' girl. We know she worked here, in your kitchens."

"I see," she said. "Just a moment please." She stood up, turned to the door, and knocked softly.

He took another look at her and noted she had a very nice figure and legs. He heard a muffled voice from behind the door and she went in. She returned a moment later, holding the door open for him.

"James Lackner, please take a seat," the man sitting at the desk said as he stood up and gestured to a chair in front of the desk. He looked to be in his early fifties; tall, with a slender build and a full head of dark neatly combed hair. He wore an expensive three-piece gray pinstriped suit that definitely looked tailored. There was a white carnation in the left lapel. A quick glance at his left hand revealed he was married.

"Miss Walton said something about a missing girl and that she worked here at the hotel?"

"That's right," Pete said. "I was hopin' to get some background on her, perhaps a look at her personnel file; maybe talk to her co-workers."

"Of course. Anything you need. What is this girl's name?"

"Catherine Paul. Works in your kitchen."

Lackner pressed a button on the intercom on the desk.

"Miss Walton," he said, leaning forward. "Please bring in the personnel file for Catherine Paul."

"Yes sir," a tinny voice sounded through the device.

"It'll just take a moment," he said, sitting back. "Can I offer you a coffee while we wait?"

"I'm good, thanks anyway," Pete said. "I'm surprised you have an Indian workin' here. Are there others?"

"Not really. Although we do employ several Negros; mostly as porters, cleaners, maids, that sort of position," he said, as if to give the impression he was a liberal minded employer.

The door opened and Miss Walton entered with a file in her hand. She stepped to the desk and passed it to Lackner.

"Thank you," he said as she turned and walked away. Pete noted Lackner watching her walk away for just a few seconds then, looking at the file, opened it and directed his attention to the couple of sheets of paper inside before passing them across to Pete.

Pete took the file and scanned the information which was mostly what he expected to find: name, address, job description and so on. He took out his notebook and wrote down her address then set the file on the desk.

"As you can see, she was hired back in the spring." Lackner made a steeple with his fingers, hands resting on the desk.

"I see her work report shows she was a good worker."

"I would assume so if she was still employed. I do not deal with personnel matters directly, so I would not know about her performance."

"Hm," Pete said. "Would it be alright I spoke to her co-workers?"

"Yes, of course. I will have Miss Walton call for a bellboy to come and take you to the kitchen."

"Thanks," Pete said, standing up.

"The chef on duty is Marcel Ducharme," Lackner said, standing up as well. "I do hope you will not take too long. The staff will be getting ready for the lunch trade, you see."

"I'll be quick. Thank you for your cooperation."

Pete left the manager's office escorted by the bellboy and made his way to the dining-room located just off the lobby to the left as you came in from outside. He was met by one of the waiters setting up the dining room tables for lunch. He eyed Pete, assessing him. The bellboy took a hasty exit.

"Sir? Do you have a reservation?"

Pete showed his ID.

"Which way to the kitchen?"

"What is the reason for…?" the waiter started to say.

"Police business," Pete said, ignoring the man's tone. "You gotta a problem with that, call the Manager. Which way?"

The man hesitated a moment then signaled for a nearby waitress to come over. She didn't look much older than eighteen.

"Miss Rafuse will take you," he said.

Pete followed the waitress to a set of double swinging doors behind a partition wall. As he neared the doors, he detected the aromas of cooking foods from beyond the doors. The waitress opened one of the doors and pointed to a man wearing a chef's cap. He thanked the young woman and went inside.

The kitchen was a beehive of white clad people working at various stations prepping food for the upcoming lunch trade. Most ignored him as he stood there for a moment before heading over to the chef. who was in a conversation with another cook and had not yet seen him approaching.

"Who are you and what do you want?" the chef asked when he finally noticed him.

"Police," Pete said, showing him his badge. "Is there someplace quiet we can talk?"

The chef turned and headed for small room in the corner with a desk in it. Marcel Ducharme was a short heavyset man in his fifties with a full rounded face and a jowl under his chin. He wore wire framed spectacles that rested on the end of his slightly narrow nose.

"What's this all about?" Ducharme asked as he closed the door. He went to the desk and sat down. Pete noted a hint of a French accent.

"I'm lookin' into a missin' girl. Accordin' to her mother, she works here at the hotel."

"There are a lot of girls and women working here. Why are you asking me about her?"

"She worked in the kitchen as a scullery."

"I see. What's her name?"

"Catherine Paul. She's twenty years old." He pulled out the picture Robie gave him and passed it to the chef. "That's her."

Ducharme took the picture and studied it for a moment before giving it back to him.

"I seem to re-call seeing her," he said.

Pete gave him a questioning look.

"I do not hire the cleaning staff or, for that matter, have any direct contact with them. That's the responsibility of the maître d'hôtel. He oversees the dining room staff: the waiters, waitresses, busboys and cleaners. Perhaps he will be better able to assist you. Now, if that is all, I have food to make ready." He stood up and opened the door.

"Thanks for your help," Pete said with just a touch of sarcasm. He left the kitchen and went in search of the maître d'hôtel in the dining room. He spotted him talking to three uniformed waiters in front of a high window looking out onto South Park Street and across to the Public Gardens. He stepped over to the men, badge in hand.

One of the waiters looked at him, alerting the maître d'hôtel who turned to face him.

He was a well-dressed man: neatly pressed black pants, white shirt and black bow tie under a waistcoat and single-breasted jacket. Pete guessed him to be in his fifties. He carried himself with an air of self-importance and a suggestion of being a fancy boy.

"Yes?" he said, dropping his eyes to look at Pete's badge.

"I'm Detective Sergeant Duncan," Pete said, putting his badge back in his pocket. "You are?"

"Steven Foyle," he answered. "What can I do for you?"

"I'm lookin' into a reported missin' woman."

"Missing woman? What on earth has that to do with me.?

"She's s'pose to work here. In the kitchen. Her name is Catherine Paul. I was told you manage all the staff in the restaurant."

"That is correct, but I'm afraid I don't know anything about this woman being missing."

"She was last seen here last Friday. You sayin' you didn't know she hadn't turned to for work?"

"As I recall, she works in the kitchen as a scrubber. I generally do not concern myself with that part of the staff. As to her not coming to work, well, it has not been reported to me so…?" he said with a shrug.

"I see. I want to ask your staff a few questions. It won't take long, Mr. Lackner has okay'd it." Pete said.

"Then by all means," Foyle said, waving a hand to the three waiters who were still standing nearby then walked off toward the entrance to the dining area.

Pete went to the three men. They were all dressed in uniforms: black trousers, white jackets, white shirts, and black bow ties. They all looked young, probably in their mid-twenties.

"Any a you fellas know this woman?" he asked when he reached them, showing the showing the picture.

One of the waiters spoke up saying, "Yeah, we know her. Works in the cleanin' room back a the kitchen. Why you askin'? She in trouble or somethin'?"

"When was the last time you saw her?"

The three looked at each other for a moment then another one said, "Last week, I think." They all nodded.

"You know if she was seein' anyone? Maybe someone workin' here?"

They shook their heads.

"Hey, now you mention it," the first one to speak said. "One of the waiters was sorta tryin' to make moves on her. You guys remember, Charlie was always tryin' to make out with her. You remember. She even made a complaint."

"Oh yeah, now I remember," another waiter said. He used ta always say somethin' 'bout wantin' to make it with an Indian."

"What's this Charlie's full name?" Pete asked.

"Charlie Wilson. Was here only a month or so."

"Whaddya mean, 'was here'?"

"Got fired 'bout a week ago. Drinkin' on the job."

"Right. Thanks for yer help. If I need to talk to you again, I'll be back. If any of you remember somethin' call the station an' ask for Detective Duncan."

Pete took down their names and addresses in his notebook before he went in search of the maître'd. He located him a few minutes later in the lobby talking with Lackner's secretary.

"...yes, of course," he said to her, taking a sheet of paper from her. "I will take care of it."

He turned and looked at Pete.

"I have a coupla quick questions then I'll get outta your hair," Pete said, still holding his notebook.

"Yes?"

"What can you tell me about a man who worked here in the dining room named Charles Wilson?"

"Oh, him," Foyle said, with a slight shake of his head. "Total incompetent. Had no experience whatsoever for waiting tables. He was discharged, oh, about a week ago. Why do you ask?"

"Do you have an address for him?" Pete asked, ignoring his question.

"No. However, I am sure you can get what you need from personnel. That would be upstairs on the mezzanine next to the Manager's office."

"While he was here, did you notice if he showed any interest in Catherine Paul or any of the female staff?"

"I wouldn't know anything about that, I'm sure. My only concern with the wait staff was their attire and quality of service. Maybe someone in the kitchen could answer that question, after all, the girl was just a scrubber and not my concern. Is that all? I must return to my duties."

"Yeah, that's it for now," Pete said, trying to keep his annoyance with the smug little man at bay. "I'll be back if anythin' comes up."

Back in the kitchen, he did a quick run through the staff while they continued their work. He didn't learn much more. However, one of the preparation cooks did say he thought he heard someone say that Paul did go out to a movie once with Wilson.

His next stop was up to the personnel office. Ten minutes later he was on his way back to the station with Wilson's employment application in his pocket.

* * *

I was back my desk riffling through several papers when Pete came into the squad room and pulled a chair close and sat down.

"How'd it go?" I asked.

"Not too bad," he said, taking out his notebook and Charles Wilson's employment application. "Seems Catherine Paul was pretty much ignored by most of the staff in the kitchen and dining room, except for one a the waiters. A guy named Charles Wilson," he said, passing over the application. "Accordin' to one of the cooks, he heard someone mention that Wilson and Paul went to a movie once. I went back an' asked the waiters if they knew anythin' 'bout this an' got nothin'."

"What did this Wilson have to say?" I asked, scanning the sheet of paper.

"Didn't talk to him. Seems he got himself fired 'bout a week ago."

"Oh?"

"Lousy waiter, accordin' to the maître d'hôtel. Plus, there were several complaints from the female staff 'bout him harassing them."

"They mention if he an' Paul...?"

258

Pete shook his head, saying, "Nothin' more than hearin' he might've takin' her out to a film. But, like I said, he was always tryin' to get it on with some of the women."

"Okay. Good work. I think you should stick with this Wilson. See what he's got to say."

"Right," Pete said. "By the way, how'd it go upstairs? Anythin' interestin'?"

"Looks like I'm back workin' with Phil an' Michael."

"No kiddin'? What's up?"

"Appears there's a gang hijacking trucks somewhere between here an' Windsor an'…"

"Let me guess," he said, interrupting me. "They need our help because they don't have the manpower or experience to deal with it."

"Somethin' like that," I said. "Look. Keep at the missing girl case but stay loose in case I need to bring you on this business."

"Okay. This mean you're goin' to be workin' down there?"

"Yeah," I said, nodding. "I'm meetin' Michael for lunch. I'll keep in touch and want you to do the same, especially if you find anythin', or the girl."

"Gotcha." Pete stood up and, taking the application form back, went to his desk.

I checked the wall clock; almost time to meet with Parks.

Chapter Three

I arrived at Naval Headquarters fifteen minutes before my meeting and went inside. The main floor was busy as usual with naval officers, WAVES, and uniformed sailors bustling about, many carrying papers or boxes. Looking around the reception area I noted that I was one of about six civilians present.

"I help you?" said a uniformed navy rating wearing the white webbing of the shore patrol and carrying a British Sten gun slung on his right shoulder.

I pulled out my security identity card that Parks had arranged for me a year before when we worked on another case; it was set behind my badge.

"Yes sir," he said, taking a step back after carefully eyeing the card and badge. "Jus' go over to da desk an' sign in."

"Thanks," I said, stepping over to a desk with a pretty young WAVE sitting behind it. She wore the single stripe around the cuff of her tunic, indicating she was a sub lieutenant.

"Yes sir?" she asked, looking up.

"Detective Robichaud," I said, showing her my police and security IDs. "I'm meetin' Lieutenant Commander Parks."

"Oh yes, he alerted me that you'd be coming in. He asked me to tell you to go down to the canteen and he would meet you there."

"Thanks." I started to turn aside when she said someone would show me the way.

"That's okay," I said. "Been there a coupla times already."

I made my way to the canteen and found an empty table in a corner with four chairs set around it. A steward dressed in whites came over as I sat down.

"Sir?' he said.

"Coffee," I said, setting my hat on the floor beside the chair. "I'm waitin' for more to join me."

"Yes sir," he said and turned back to the kitchen.

Ten minutes later, I saw Michael Parks come in followed by Phil Mulroney.

"Phil," I said when they reached the table.

He nodded and pulled out a wooden chair and sat down. "How's Pete doing? Still enjoying the honeymoon?" he asked.

"What do you think?"

Phil just smiled.

Pete had recently married a woman we met on one of our first major cases back in '39. Her name was Agnes – Aggie to her friends – Sullivan. A lovely woman who worked at one of the sheds down at the southern docks. I had the pleasure of standing as his best man with a couple of beat cops from his early days on the force as ushers. It was a big do with Morrison and plenty of cops in attendance in spite of the rationing restrictions.

"How's the spy business?" I asked. "Any more Gerries givin' you grief?"

"No. I figure the Abwehr got the word that it wasn't worth losing more agents. These days our problems in that regard are coming from Nazi sympathizers and those against the war. But that's another story. Michael tells me that you've been brought up to date on the hijacking business."

"More or less, yeah," I said. "We've known about the problem in connection with several investigations we're runnin' into the black market trade in stolen goods."

"The problem has become a major concern for us since, whoever is running this operation, seems to know when and what shipments to target," Michael said, joining in.

"You thinkin' someone is passin' information?" I asked.

"Looks like it," Phil stated. "I've got two men working on it. So far, nothing."

"Where they look'?"

"Well, the obvious place to start is the docks but we haven't been able to narrow it down to a specific dock or set of docks."

262

"And now with this last heist," Michael added, "it may be even more difficult."

"Because the hit happened between Truro an' the port," I said. "Comin' from the other direction."

Phil nodded, saying, "That's why we think there might be some sort of organization behind it."

"Makes sense," I said. "So, what do you want me to do?"

"If there is an organized criminal gang operating in our area we need to find out as fast as possible and shut it down," Michael said.

"What we need you to do," Phil told me, "is to tackle this from your end and try to identify who they are and where they are operating from. Then, we can take over and make the arrests."

"Don't your people have better investigative tools at your disposal than I have?"

"We do, and they are all open for you to use. And before you say anything more, we asked for your help because of your background and experience dealing with organized crime back in Boston."

"Thanks, I suppose. But I don't know what you think I did back then, I mean, I was just a beat cop, but if I can help, I will."

"Good man," Michael said, signaling for one of the uniformed stewards. "Let's eat, then we can go back to the office."

As I said before, Headquarters always managed to lay their hands on an ample supply of the best of the available rations for their canteen; today was no exception. Today it was a boiled dinner of corned beef and cabbage with turnips and carrots. We finished off the meal with hot apple cobbler and coffee.

Later, back upstairs in Phil's office, he passed me a stack of reports covering the last half dozen thefts saying these were the ones that appeared to be connected to the same thieves. We agreed to meet up in three hours to discuss them. He also arranged for me to meet and talk to the men he assigned to the case. Halfway through them it became clear he had some good people under him working on the case. The notes were well organized and carefully documented; however, they did not point to any conclusive end and seemed to raise more questions than answers.

I was almost near the end of the last report when Phil knocked on the door of the small office I was assigned.

"How's it going?" he asked, stepping in and sitting down.

"You got good people here," I answered, holding up the report. "Good detail. Well thought out."

"Thanks. I got lucky and managed to get several good investigators from Upper Canada posted down here for the duration.

They have plenty of criminal work behind them, especially Special Constable Carl Watkins. Worked the organized crime unit in Quebec City for a year before the war."

"I'd like to meet him an' get his thoughts on this business."

"I'll set it up. He's away on an assignment up in Sydney at the moment and is due back in a couple of days. So, I take it you are thinking there is a mob connection?"

"Would make sense," I said.

"Remember a year or so back we had that business with the dead man up in Greenbank and we uncovered a pilfering ring involving the Corse Unione?"

"That's the criminal organization operating mostly out of Southern France, northwest Africa and French Indochina, if I remember. They deal primarily in the opium trade out of Southeast Asia, as I recall.

That's right," Phil said. "Good memory. Anyway, their organization rivals the Sicilian Mafia in Italy, although according to our contacts overseas they have been collaborating with them and their heroin business."

I said. "You tellin me...?"

"No," he said, cutting me off. "We have no evidence they are operating down here. I only mention them because when they showed up in Montreal a few years ago our intelligence division learned they've partnered with one or more local crime

265

families. If this hijacking operation is being controlled from Quebec, then it's possible they might be involved."

"Jesus," I said again.

"It gets worse, if it is these people, we have to be very careful. They have a reputation for being extremely violent."

"But they're not here?" I asked.

He shook his head, saying, "We're thinking that a local gang is running the operation on this end for whoever is behind it in Montreal."

I shook my head.

"I don't think so. Sure, there's a few I could name who'd have the mettle to try somethin' this big, but they wouldn't have the manpower or the network to get rid of the goods. Mind you, if it is the mob outta Montreal, they'd definitely be lookin' for someone local to use, mostly for labour an' muscle. Someone who'd know the lay of the land, so to speak."

"So, what do you suggest as a course of action?"

"I'll make some inquiries. Maybe I'll pick up somethin'. Also, I'm thinkin' of bringin' Aggie in on this. She's ideally placed to pick up any rumors, and she helped us out before."

Pete's wife worked on the docks at pier twenty-four as a records clerk. A smart and resourceful woman and honest. Something clicked between her and Pete and a relationship soon developed. One of the few good things to come out of this war so far.

"Good thinking," Phil said. "Meanwhile, I'll get in touch with our people in Montreal and Quebec City; see if they've picked on any increase in black market activity. You're right about the disposal of the goods. They have to be going somewhere and we haven't heard about any of it hitting the streets here so far."

"We haven't heard or picked up on any of these goods showing up on the street either but that doesn't mean they aren't out there. Like I said, I'll make a few calls to some people I know who've got their ear open to what's goin' on. If there's somethin' they'll know."

"These people, they're reliable?"

I shrugged, saying, "As much as any lowlife is, but I used them before an' I can lean on them if necessary. You know how it goes with informants."

"Unfortunately, I do. But that's the job, right?"

"Right. Now, if you got nothin' else..."

"Yeah, okay," Phil said, getting up from the chair. "I'll set up that meeting with Watkins. Let me know if you get anything and how you make out with Aggie. Think Pete'll mind?"

"I don't think so. By the way, can you arrange a car for me?"

"Sure thing," he said. "You know where to go."

I got up, grabbed my hat and coat, and headed out. My first stop after I signed out a car from the carpool was a pool parlor up on Gottingen Street. It was a local hangout for the blacks in the neighborhood and many of the petty criminals working in the city. I wanted to find Chet Munroe, an ex-cop who had left the force under a cloud. He worked the Gottingen Street area up around Stadacona, his onetime patrol beat. He wasn't exactly 'dirty', but he did mess up with a known prostitute that led to his dismissal from the force. He and I had a sort of relationship which began back when I joined the force. These days he was driving a cab and shilling for a local bootlegger. Last I heard he was also pimping for a couple of women. He was also one of my main sources of information about what was happening in the city.

I got lucky and spotted another one of my informers standing on the corner of Gerrish Street talking with two women. As I neared the corner, I slowed down and tapped the horn. He glanced at me as I turned the corner and stopped half a block away. I watched in the side mirror to make sure he saw me and came up to the car. When he reached the car, he opened the rear right passenger door and slid onto the seat. I looked at him in the rearview mirror.

He was furtively looking over his shoulder out the rear window.

"Relax," I said. "No one saw you."

"Cain't be too careful," he said, slouching into the corner of the seat.

His name was Curtis Paris. A fifty something black man. He lived in the area, at a flop on Maynard Street, last I heard. I arrested him for the first time back in '35 for petty theft. He was about to do a six-month stretch in Rockhead Prison when he first offered to turn over on some car thieves operating at the time in exchange for a break. I managed to talk the Crown Prosecutor into giving him a suspended sentence after I broke up the thieves' operation. He'd been one of my informers since then, although I usually had to look hard to find him.

"This won't take long," I said. "Whaddya hear 'bout stolen goods comin' into the market?"

"Yeah. I heard there's some prime shit showin' up," he said.

"An'?"

"Dat's it."

"Who's bringin' it in?"

"Word I git is dey ain't local."

"Nothin' else?"

"Nope," he said, shaking his head. "Dat's all I got. I hear it ain't good for a body to ax too many questions."

I considered what he told me. I wasn't about to put him in harm's way; he was too good a contact.

"Right," I said. "Thanks. Send me word if you pick up anythin' on who these people are, okay? An' if you can't reach me, talk to Pete."

"Sure t'ing, Robbie. Count on it."

"One more thing," I said as he reached for the door handle. "Have you seen Munroe 'round the parlor?"

"Nope. Ain't been 'round fer a cupla days. Last I heard, he's been up 'round the shipyards hustlin' his wimmin. There's a Yankee boat in fer fixin' up. Good chance to score summa dem green backs."

"Thanks." I slipped him a five-dollar bank note before he exited the car.

I headed back to Gottingen Street thinking over what Paris told me. It appeared some of the goods taken by the hijackers were making their way into the city's underground market. Question was: Who's bringing the stuff in and who's distributing it?

I turned down North Street then left onto Barrington. I was headed for a blind-pig-run-out of a house on Union Street up in the north end. We had shut the place down a few times before it was decided to leave it alone since there were never any problems at the house.

It was run by Marg Reynolds, an overweight woman in her sixties. She was a widow who lost her husband while he was fishing on the Grand Banks off Newfoundland back in '28. She ran a quiet operation and was liked by the area residents and workers from the shipyard who made up her main trade and who affectionately called her Ma. Rumor has it that one night last year some asshole with a skin full in him tried something and a half dozen of her regulars put him right. He was discharged from the Victoria General Hospital six weeks later.

I parked the car a block away and got out, choosing to walk the rest of the way. Reynold's place wasn't hard to find; there were always a dozen or so men milling around the front stoop. As I neared the house, I eyed the street, looking for Munroe's cab. No luck. I did spot a woman talking to a couple of men in work overalls about five doors up the street. I recognized her as Carla, one of Munroe's doxies. As I approached her, she said something to the men who quickly walked away.

"Hey Detective," she said. "Long time no see."

"Carla," I said. "How're tricks?"

"Funny you should ask. You finally interested?" Then quickly added, "Just kidding."

Carla was an attractive woman, probably in her late twenties or early thirties: light brown shoulder length hair, fair complexion, nice body with round hips and perky breasts. She been selling herself almost since the start of the war. I heard somewhere she got married to a soldier a while back. He was overseas now.

"Right. I'm looking for Munroe. Seen him?" I knew she sometimes let him pimp for her.

"Yeah," she said. "He's been around. Last I saw him was about a half hour ago. I think he was making a run for Max. Should be back soon. Want I should tell him you're looking for him?"

Max Howell was a local area hustler who pushed bootlegged whiskey for a family on the eastern shore, Jeddore, I think.

"I'll hang 'round a bit, thanks anyway," I said, heading back to my car.

After an hour of waiting, I decided to head back to the station and check in with Pete to see if he was making any headway of the missing woman and to bounce my idea of using Aggie.

He wasn't in but there was a message from Curtis Paris. It said he wanted to meet me at the usual place at five o'clock. The usual place was on a side street beside the Halifax Armories. I checked my watch; it read four-fifteen.

I made it up to the Armories and parked by the coal delivery chute leading down into the dark brown stone building.

It was built like a small fortress or redoubt. The blocks of reddish-brown rock looked like they had to weigh several hundred pounds each. Narrow windows were cut into to the wall. A relic from before the last war.

I spotted Paris rounding the corner and heading towards the chute. I flipped my lights which got his attention. When he reached the car, he got in on the passenger side front seat.

"Whaddya got?" I asked without any preamble.

"No sooner ya split in comes dis yahoo. He starts flashing a wad wud choke a mule an' starts runnin' 'is mouth. I git ta thinkin' dis a dumb shit mark, so I tries ta take a bite. Turns out he ain't no rube. Sez he's lookin' for sum hired muscle fer a job."

"What kind a job?"

"Didn't say, but it musta been shady 'cause I git a glimpse inside his jacket an' spotted da gun he was carryin'. Anyways, I weren't innerested in any action wit guns."

"Did you catch a name?"

"Jake MacDonald."

I knew Jake MacDonald. Ran one of the gangs operating just outside the city up in Kline Heights, just far enough out of my reach. He was mostly a small-time operator, running booze and a small black market in stolen goods. He wasn't known to be a hard case, although I suspect he was behind a number of nasty assaults, mainly muggings.

Word on him was that he sometimes did heavy work if the price was right. He leaned on people, hard. I heard he liked hurting people.

"How many people did he hire?"

He shrugged, saying, "Don't know. He sez anyone innerested to meet him at Kelly's ole place at ten."

The place he was referring to was a gin mill down on Inglis Street used to be run by an Irish hood with IRA connections who I shut down back in thirty-nine. Last I heard a couple of women from out of town were running a discrete sex shop there now.

"Thanks," I said and handed him a ten-dollar bank note. "Call if you get any more, especially if you hear anythin' 'bout any incomin' goods."

"Gotcha," he said as he opened the door and hoofed it back down the lane.

I started the car and headed back to the station to meet up with Pete.

* * *

There was still plenty of time, so Pete headed back out to look for Charles Wilson. According to his employment record, he lived in the south end on Smith Street near Inglis. It was a short dead-end street with ten rundown crappy wooden boarding houses on it. Most of the residents were men working for the rail yard or on the docks. There had been a few complaints called in from this area by residents. Mostly, they had to do with squabbles between tenants and landlords over poor conditions or high rents; both were becoming more frequent throughout the city as available space was at a premium.

Wilson lived at number six. It was a two-story building with a flat roof and narrow windows across the side facing the street. Pete parked at the curb across from the wooden door and got out. He crossed to the house and rapped on the door. After several moments a man opened the door.

"Yeah?," he said in a deep, raspy voice. "Whaddya want?"

He was in his sixties and bald. He wore a dingy, faded white shirt tucked into a pair of dungarees held up by a wide black leather belt. His bloated belly spilled over the top of the pants. Pete noted the two long faded tattoos; one on each forearm.

"I'm lookin' for Charles Wilson," Pete said, extracting his wallet and flashing his badge.

"Yeah? What's the little shit done?"

"Is he in?"

"Naw. I booted 'im out. Couldn't pay da rent."

"When was that?"

"Last week an' b'fore ya ask, no, I don't know where he went. Maybe ya shud ask dat bit a skirt he was with."

"A girl you say?" Pete said. "Tell me 'bout her.?"

"Ain't much ta tell," the man said. "She started comin' 'round, I don't know, maybe three weeks back. None a my business who my tenants are shaggin', long's dey pay the rent."

Pete pulled the picture of Catherine Paul out and showed it to him.

"This her?"

He took the picture and brought up closer to his eyes then nodded. "Yeah. Dat's her."

"Just to make sure I got this straight, you're sayin' this girl has been staying here with Charles Wilson for at least the last few weeks, that right?"

"Can't rightly say she was stayin' with him, but she was definitely here quite a bit."

"Okay, thanks for your help." Pete put everything back in his coat pocket and headed for the car, thinking Robie might not be too happy when he made his report.

Visit link below to purchase Robie's War

https://bookswelove.net/doucette-h-paul/

Also published by BWL Publishing Inc.

H. Paul Doucette is 74 years old and lives in Dartmouth, Nova Scotia, Canada. He has lived and worked in many countries throughout a varied career in International Transportation. In the course of his life he have attended University and an Art College. He has dedicated the last twelve years to developing as a novelist.

The John Robichaud series is set in Halifax, Nova Scotia during the Second War World and follows a police detective. This series, consisting of six stories, is currently in print with a Canadian publisher, BWL Publishing in Alberta, Canada.